Carrion of the gods

A TRIO killer raised a Chinese *fu* hatchet and hurled it at Encizo. The Cuban weaved away, but the handle tagged his shoulder.

The Phoenix member grimaced at his brush with death. He triggered the machine pistol, and 9mm shockers shredded the hatchet man's chest.

The silence that followed was brief; shooting resumed upstairs, but the fighting in the worship hall was over. Encizo gazed at the incense smoke wafting before the bronze Buddha's face. As he watched, the statue seemed to shake its head, as if saddened by the bloodshed.

That makes two of us, the Cuban thought grimly.

Mack Bolan's
PHOENIX FORCE

PHOENIX FORCE

Welcome to the Feast

Gar Wilson

A GOLD EAGLE BOOK FROM

W RLDWIDE

TORONTO · NEW YORK · LONDON · PARIS
AMSTERDAM · STOCKHOLM · HAMBURG
ATHENS · MILAN · TOKYO · SYDNEY

First edition May 1985

ISBN 0-373-61317-2

Special thanks and acknowledgment to
William Fieldhouse for his contributions to this work.

1

Lt. Timothy Martin steered the Coast Guard powerboat as he glanced about at the monotonous darkness. A blanket of clouds blotted out most of the stars overhead, and the lights of the vessel did little to penetrate the shadows of night.

The Pacific rippled passively along the bow of the boat. The ocean was gentle tonight, but Martin knew the sea to be unpredictable. It could become wild and violent in a matter of minutes. The lieutenant did not like the look of the clouds; a change in weather meant a change in the sea.

Martin would have almost welcomed a small typhoon. Almost. Cruising along the California coast between Point Arena and Bodega Bay at three in the morning is about as exciting as watching a training film on cleaning toilet bowls. However, the Coast Guard's main function is patrolling the waters to assist distressed civilians at sea. Amateur sailors can get in trouble anytime, anywhere. Thus the "graveyard patrol" was necessary.

Still, Martin wished he was home in bed with his wife, Anna. Duty can be a real bummer. Martin loved the sea and he enjoyed his job, which he regarded as a vital and important service. But he also loved Anna and the kids. He looked forward to spending the weekend with his family, taking a pleasure cruise down to San Diego.

"Lieutenant!" the familiar voice of CPO Ormond called from the port side. "Rivera has just picked up something on sonar. Looks like a ship only about a mile southwest of our position.''

"A ship?" Martin frowned as he reached for a pair of Tasco 8x40 binoculars. "I haven't seen or heard anything. Maybe Rivera picked up a whale.''

"Then it's a big bastard,'' Ormond replied as he slipped off his white cap to scratch his balding head. "About sixty feet long. Wouldn't want to run into a fish that big. Might piss 'im off enough to attack us. Sucker that big could knock this boat upside down.''

"Whales aren't fish,'' Martin commented as he scanned the ocean through his field glass. "And you've seen *Moby Dick* too many times, Charlie.''

"Maybe,'' the chief petty officer grunted. "But I figure legends about whales gotta have some truth to 'em.''

"Don't bet on it,'' Martin said. "Besides, we've got sonar and whales have a kind of natural sonar system, too. I don't think we have to worry about a collision.''

"Sure hope you're right, sir.'' Ormond sighed, still not convinced.

"Forget the whale, Charlie,'' the lieutenant rasped as a shape materialized via the lens of his binoculars. "I found our mystery ship.''

Martin stared at the big black vessel. A cargo ship, it was at least sixty feet long and rode the waves at a casual pace. Although undoubtedly equipped with engines, the ship was powered by a great black sail. Not a single light shone from the black vessel as it crept along through the night.

"Maybe their engines are out of order and the generator is shot,'' Martin mused, though he did not believe this for a moment.

"And they don't have any flashlights on board?'' Ormond remarked dryly. "If that tub is in distress they'd send up a flare or something. I don't like it, sir. A black ship sneaking around at this hour. Sure seems suspicious, if you ask me, Lieutenant.''

"I agree," Martin said. "Tell Sparks to get on the radio and contact headquarters. I want some backup out here on the double. If that ship is crawling with modern-day pirates, I don't want us to have to take them on by ourselves. This is a Coast Guard vessel, not a naval destroyer.''

"Pirates, sir?" Ormond raised his shaggy eyebrows.

"Not as incredible as it might sound," the lieutenant replied. "Piracy still goes on, you know. Look at all those tuna boats that have been hijacked between Mexico and San Diego.''

"But this is mighty far north for seagoing *bandidos*," Ormond mused. "Probably homegrown troublemakers.''

"Let's not jump to conclusions," Martin urged. "That ship might be perfectly innocent. But I don't want to take any chances.''

"Yes, sir," the CPO agreed. "I'll tell Sparks to radio HQ pronto.''

"And issue .45s to the men," Martin added. "Just in case.''

"Aye, aye, Lieutenant," Ormond replied earnestly.

Martin kept the Coast Guard boat a safe distance from the black ship. He had no intention of getting closer until reinforcements arrived. The vessel slowly circled the area. Whoever was on board the ship could certainly see the lights on the powerboat, probably hear the engines, too. Anyone with binoculars could clearly read the Coast Guard legend painted on its side. Why did they refuse to acknowledge the presence of the Coast Guard vessel? What were they trying to hide?

Another possibility occurred to Martin. Maybe there

was no one on board the black ship. He had not seen anyone moving about the decks of the ominous dark vessel. Was it deserted? If so, what happened to the crew?

Lieutenant Martin considered himself to be a logical, down-to-earth fellow. Yet he could not prevent bizarre notions from slipping into his thoughts. Old legends of *The Flying Dutchman* and other ghost ships. Rumors of spooky incidents in the so-called Bermuda Triangle. Ships and planes disappearing without a trace. Vessels found deserted, the crews mysteriously vanished.

Bullshit, Martin told himself. There are no such things as ghosts, and those stories about the Bermuda Triangle are just a bunch of crap. Besides, they were off the coast of California, not Bermuda. Still, the sight of the black ship caused a shiver to crawl up the young officer's spine like a centipede.

Lieutenant Martin's fears would prove to be all too real.

SIX FIGURES SWAM toward the Coast Guard boat. They easily paddled their flipper-clad feet to propel themselves through the water. Thin columns of bubbles rose from the air tanks strapped to their backs as the frogmen drew closer. The pointman held a waterproof, high-intensity flashlight. The beam cut through the darkness to find the hull of the powerboat.

The pointman gestured toward the belly of the Coast Guard vessel as it passed overhead. Another frogman nodded and raised a Surudoi spear gun. He aimed the weapon carefully, following the movement of the boat. Then the frogman pulled the trigger, and a powerful CO_2 cartridge launched a spear.

The missile knifed through the water and struck the hull of the powerboat. The spearhead itself was a stubby aluminum tube with a steel pressure plate at the tip; the tube contained four ounces of potassium chlorate, a simple explosive, easily made and extremely volatile. The charge exploded on impact, and most of the blast traveled upward to burst the skin of the hull.

"What the hell was that?" Lieutenant Martin demanded when he heard the explosion from the belly of the boat and felt the vessel tremble violently and twist about in the water.

"Something blew up aft of starboard," Ormond shouted in reply. "I don't know what happened, but we've got water pouring into the companionway, sir."

"Christ," Martin muttered as he killed the engine. "Great time for something like this to happen. Get Rivera on repairs. I don't expect miracles, but tell him to do what he can. Tell Sparks to get out a Mayday, if he hasn't done it already."

"Aye, aye, sir," Ormond's voice echoed from the interior of the boat.

Martin bounced a fist against the wheel in anger. He gathered up his binoculars to see if anything had changed on the decks of the black ship. The lieutenant froze when he saw figures climb over the handrail at the port side of the Coast Guard vessel. Their faces were covered by the tinted single lens of their diving masks. Water dripped from black wetsuits as the invaders' finned feet slapped the deck.

"We're under attack!" Martin shouted. "Arm yourselves...."

One of the invaders swiftly yanked a four-pointed object from a leather pouch on his weighted belt and hurled it at Martin. The officer screamed when the star-shaped weapon struck his chest and pierced cloth to stab flesh. Martin threw himself to the deck as another throwing star whistled past his head to sail overboard and into the ocean beyond.

"Get the lead out, damn it!" Ormond bellowed. "This ain't no fucking drill!"

The CPO charged up the companionway, a .45-caliber 1911A1 Government Issue Colt in his fist. "Shit," Ormond muttered when he saw three black shapes at the stern of the boat. He raised his pistol and thumbed off the safety catch.

Three arms swung in unison, hurling a trio of throwing stars. Sharp steel teeth bit into Ormond's chest and face before he could trigger his weapon. The CPO squeezed the trigger of his pistol in a reflex action, but the bullet rocketed harmlessly into the darkness.

Three more death stars spun across the deck and slammed into the chief petty officer. The .45 dropped from his hand as steel stabbed his biceps. The other stars pierced his chest, and Ormond collapsed against the risers of the companionway. As he went down, Ormond saw a black-suited invader rush forward and draw a long knife from his belt.

The man pounced on Ormond's supine body and plunged the knife in the wounded man's chest, driving the slanted steel point into the noncom's heart. The killer grunted with satisfaction as he felt his victim tremble in a final death spasm.

"¡Que la chigada!" Rivera snarled as he aimed his Colt autoloader at the assassin.

The killer glanced up as the big pistol boomed. A 230-grain hard-ball slug shattered the lens of his face mask. The bullet split bone and burrowed into the invader's brain, and the assassin slumped across the corpse of CPO Ormond. Rivera advanced, holding the pistol in both hands.

"Come on, you fuckers!" the young Chicano shouted. "You wanta fight? Come on, man!"

An object suddenly whirled around the top of the entrance to the companionway. Rivera barely saw a blur of motion before sharp metal punched into his torso, just above the solar plexus. He screamed and glanced down at the crescent-shaped blade buried in his chest. A length of chain attached to the blade extended beyond the companionway.

A black-suited killer on the main deck yanked the chain hard, and Rivera was pulled across the threshold. Another assassin had ripped open a waterproof rubber sack to remove a 9mm Nambu automatic, and he promptly shot Rivera twice in the back of the head.

The gunman slithered into the companionway, pistol held ready. Two of his comrades followed, each quickly scooping up a .45 Colt from the lifeless fingers of the slain Coast Guard sailors. The trio of killers crept through the companionway on bare feet, weapons poised for action.

Petty Officer Second Class David Sparks sat by the radio, Colt automatic in one hand, and desperately transmitted a Mayday call. A black shape danced past the entrance of Sparks's cabin, and Sparks hastily fired his .45 without taking time to aim. The bullet plowed into a wall instead of striking human flesh.

Sparks's arm rose with the recoil of the big-caliber pistol, and before he could lower it, the invader poked a Nambu around the corner and sent two 115-grain flat-nosed parabellum rounds smashing into the young officer's rib cage. Sparks dropped his pistol and crashed to the floor. Another killer triggered a confiscated .45 and pumped a third round into the wounded man's chest.

"Delta Five this is Headquarters," a voice crackled from the radio. "Do you read me? Over?"

The gunmen trained their pistols on the radio and opened fire. Bullets struck metal and plastic, reducing the radio to a tangle of wires and shards of plastic. One of the assassins took a Soviet-made F-1 grenade from his belt and reached for the pin. His partner placed a hand to his arm to stop him.

"*Ee-eh,*" he whispered. "*Okimas, Hirto-san. Okimas.*"

LIEUTENANT MARTIN CRAWLED along the starboard side of the patrol boat. He had pulled the star-shaped weapon from his chest and was astonished when he recognized the object. He did not know what it was called, but he had seen such weapons before on the old kung fu television series. The lieutenant had thought those throwing stars were ridiculous at the time, but he did not feel like laughing now with two holes in his chest and bloodstains on his shirt.

A pair of bare feet approached Lieutenant Martin and he gazed up at two legs clad in black rubber. A lone invader stood before him. The killer had stripped off his face mask, and the hardness of his almond-shaped eyes was as menacing as the long-bladed knife in his fist.

As Martin hauled himself erect, his heart was racing with terror. He tried to remember what he had been taught during a ten-hour self-defense course he had taken three years ago. The instructors had made it look easy to take a knife away from an opponent. It sure as hell did not seem easy now.

The Oriental glanced down at the crimson blotch on Martin's shirt. He noticed the lieutenant was not armed. The invader nodded, his features as expressionless as a statue's. He slid the knife into a belt sheath and raised empty hands, fingers poised like the talons of a bird of prey.

Karate, Martin thought as he balled his fists, teeth clenched as pain shot through his chest. Martin had heard conflicting stories about Oriental martial arts. Some said it was all theatrical crap. Others claimed a black belt could kill a man with his bare hands. All Martin knew was the guy was offering him something close to a fair fight. At least as close as he could expect under the circumstances.

But Martin did not intend to fight like a gentleman. He had once heard a karate guy is no match for a street fighter because the martial-arts experts figure their opponents will fight by the rules. Martin feinted a punch and swung a foot at his enemy's groin.

The Oriental's left hand swung low and chopped the inside of Martin's ankle to deflect the kick. His right fist shot out, ramming knuckles into the lieutenant's lower abdomen. A karate war cry mingled with the sound of flesh smashing into flesh. The Oriental slammed the heel of a palm across the side of Martin's face, and the stiff blow sent him reeling. A kick plowed into the Coast Guard officer's solar plexus. Martin felt as if his lungs had collapsed. He fell to his knees, certain that the kick had stopped his heart.

Lieutenant Martin's assumption was correct.

He was already dying when the Oriental chopped the side of a hand across the nape of his neck. The seventh vertebra cracked. The shock to the lieutenant's spinal cord rendered him unconscious. Martin was dead before his assassin stomped a heel on the base of his skull.

The roar of huge rotor blades slashing through the sky betrayed the approach of a Bell HH-1K helicopter, and soon a Coast Guard chopper was hovering overhead. The powerful beam of a searchlight scanned the area as the whirlybird shifted in the sky. The light traveled across the water to the black ship and caught the motion of a dozen figures darting about the deck of the cargo vessel. One group of men were hauling a bulky object shrouded by a large canvas tarp.

"This is the Coast Guard," a voice boomed from the chopper's loudspeaker. "We order you to identify ourself at once!"

The crew of the black ship removed the tarp to uncover a Type 41 light machine gun mounted on a bipod. A man sat immediately behind the rig and trained it on the Bell. He opened fire. A stream of tracer rounds sliced through the gloom as the machine gun pelted the chopper with .30-caliber devastation.

High-velocity slugs pierced the skin of the copter. Bullets punched through Plexiglas and ripped into the pilot's body. The chopper jockey convulsed in agony, pulling the collective and cyclic controls to the right. His feet slipped from the rudder, and the whirlybird swung out of control and pivoted in the sky like a wounded eagle.

Another volley of machine-gun fire ripped into the disabled aircraft and punctured the chopper's fuel tank. Bullets sparked against metal, igniting the gasoline. The tank exploded, turning the chopper into a fireball, a mininova in the night sky.

As the burning wreckage plunged into the sea, a cheer rose from the black ship. But the celebration lasted for scant seconds; the crew of the vessel had much work to do before the night was over.

2

"Well, fellas," Hal Brognola told the five men at the conference table in the Stony Man war room. "We've got a real mess for you this time."

"So what else is new?" Rafael Encizo asked dryly.

Although in his mid-forties, Encizo appeared to be ten years younger. He was a physical fitness enthusiast with a muscular physique and handsome dark features. A native-born Cuban, Encizo had formerly been a freedom fighter against Castro's Communist regime. He had been at the Bay of Pigs invasion—or perhaps one should call it the Bay of Pigs fiasco.

The Communists captured Encizo and took him to El Principe, Castro's infamous political prison, where he was starved, beaten and tortured. But no amount of physical abuse could break Rafael Encizo. One day a guard was careless. He underestimated Encizo, assuming the prisoner was too weak and exhausted to present any threat. It was the last mistake he ever made. Encizo broke his neck and escaped from El Principe.

Encizo fled to the United States and became a naturalized citizen. For two decades he drifted from job to job. He worked as a scuba instructor, an insurance investigator and even dived for sunken treasure off the coast of Bermuda. Although Encizo's impressive array of skills more than qualified him for any of these ventures, none truly satisfied the bold Cuban. Then Rafael Encizo was recruited into Phoenix Force.

Phoenix Force had been created as a special antiterrorist unit under the superb supervision of Stony Man. Hal Brognola was the chief of operations and the go-between for the organization and the President of the United States. Stony Man had originally been formed to make use of the phenomenal combat skills and experience of Mack Bolan, better known as the Executioner.

Bolan had taken on the Mafia virtually single-handed and had crushed the czars of organized crime. He was an ideal choice to command the new war against the most alarming and ruthless enemy of civilization in the history of mankind—international terrorism. Brognola and the Executioner, under the new identity of Col. John Phoenix, had created Stony Man for this purpose, and they personally selected the five men of Phoenix Force. They were looking for five of the best-trained commandos and most experienced antiterrorists in the world. They found them.

Col. Yakov Katzenelenbogen had been selected as the unit commander of Phoenix Force. The eldest of the elite fighting unit, Katz resembled a middle-aged college professor. In fact, the former Israeli Mossad intelligence officer was a scholar with degrees in archaeology, language studies and military science. He was also one of the most experienced combat veterans and espionage agents in the world.

As a teenager, Yakov had joined the underground resistance and fought the Nazis in Europe. Since most of his family perished in Hitler's death camps, Katz moved on to Palestine and participated in Israel's war for independence. Years later he was nearly killed in the Six Day War, and his right arm was wounded beyond repair. The limb had to be amputated at the elbow, but this did not stop Katz from continuing the general fight against destruction and tyranny.

Thanks to a cooperative effort with Western allies in Europe and the United States in the war against Communist espionage and international terrorism, Mossad occasionally "lent" Katz to other intelligence networks. He served with the American CIA, the British SIS, the West German BND and the French Sûreté.

Katz now sat across from Encizo at the conference table. The Cuban watched Yakov tear open a pack of Camel Lights with the steel hooks of the prosthetic device attached to the stump of his right arm. The Israeli used the metal talons to nimbly pluck a single cigarette from the pack. There was nothing clumsy about the way Katz handled that prosthesis. The hooks could also be lethal weapons at close quarters.

David McCarter was seated next to the Israeli. A fox-faced Englishman with a tall, lean physique, McCarter was a veteran of the British SAS. He had seen action in Northern Ireland, Oman, Vietnam and even served in a covert "police action" in Hong Kong. McCarter also participated in Operation Nimrod, the fabulous 1980 SAS raid on the Iranian embassy in London.

McCarter was a superb fighting man and an ace pilot who could fly anything from a hang glider to a Boeing 747. He was a champion pistol marksman, an accomplished mountaineer and an expert in virtually every form of commando warfare. The Briton could handle himself in the jungles of Southeast Asia or the streets of Belfast with equal ease.

McCarter had devoted his life to developing combat skills because he thrived on adventure. The battlefield was McCarter's favorite element, and if he had been less principled, he would have become a mercenary. But the Stony Man operations provided plenty of opportunity for adventure, and McCarter and Phoenix Force were perfect for each other.

Gary Manning sipped black coffee as he waited for Brognola to continue the briefing. A muscular Canadian, Manning was one of the best demolitions experts in the business. He could handle any explosive from blackpowder to plastique. He could blow up the basement of a house without rattling the china in the cabinets upstairs.

Manning had been a lieutenant in the Canadian Army Corps of Engineers. Like McCarter, he had also been in Vietnam as a "special observer" although Manning spent more than a year in Southeast Asia, attached to the Fifth Special Forces. A superb rifle sharpshooter, Manning became an expert sniper as well as a deadly demolitions pro. His courage under fire earned him the Silver Star, and he was one of the few Canadian citizens to receive this decoration from the United States armed forces.

After he returned from Nam, the Royal Canadian Mounted Police enlisted Manning into their covert intelligence department.

Manning served with the RCMP intel office until 1981 when a scandal about alleged abuses of power put the Mounties out of the espionage business. The Canadian Security Intelligence Service attempted to draft Manning into an administrative job, but he refused and turned his attention to the world of business and more personal pursuits. He quickly became a security consultant and junior executive for North American International, but when Stony Man offered him a new opportunity to take on the dragons of terrorism, the Canadian juggernaut eagerly accepted.

The fifth and final member of Phoenix Force was Calvin James. A tall, lanky black man, James was a graduate of the school of hard knocks in the ghetto of the south side of Chicago. At seventeen, he joined the Navy to see the world—but the U.S. military world at that time was defined as Southeast Asia. He pursued an interest in medicine and chemistry and became a hospital corpsman before eventually being accepted into an elite Sea, Air and Land team.

As a SEAL, James was trained in small arms, parachuting, hand-to-hand combat and all manner of underwater warfare and demolitions. He had ample time to develop these skills during two and a half years in Vietnam.

When James returned to the States, he hoped to continue his medical training via the GI bill. But after his sister died from an overdose of heroin and his mother was murdered by unknown assailants, he joined the San Francisco Police Department and soon became a member of the Special Weapons and Tactics team.

James was actually involved in a SWAT operation when Phoenix Force shanghaied him to meet with Brognola at Stony Man headquarters. He agreed to assist Phoenix in a mission against the insidious Black Alchemist terrorists, and he'd remained with Phoenix Force ever since. With five missions under his belt, Calvin James was a full-fledged member of the unit.

Encizo, Katz, McCarter, Manning and James constituted the most highly skilled commando strike force ever assembled.

"Okay, gentlemen," Brognola began, "three days ago a Coast Guard patrol boat and one of their helicopters were destroyed off the coast of California. Eight Guardsmen were killed."

"That was reported on the national news," Manning said. "I think they called it a 'freak accident that is under investigation.' I take it sabotage was involved?"

"Nobody is quite sure what happened," Brognola replied, lighting a cigar. "The patrol boat and the helicopter were both blown to pieces. However, the Coast Guard headquarters had received a request for assistance from the boat about half an hour earlier that night. Apparently the patrol watch had spotted a mysterious cargo ship sailing around without any lights showing. No legend or identifying markings, either.''

"The chopper was sent to assist the boat?'' James asked.

"That's right,'' the Fed confirmed. "But the patrol boat had radioed a Mayday distress call by then. Said their craft was leaking. Then the radio went dead. The copter showed up, reported seeing the black ship below. That was the last anybody heard of them, too.''

"Doesn't sound like a bloody accident to me,'' McCarter commented as he rose from his chair and began to pace. The Briton was a bundle of nervous energy and could never sit still for long.

"It wasn't an accident,'' the Fed confirmed. "The chopper was shot down. Some of the parts of the helicopter were salvaged. A few segments had been punctured by .30-caliber machine-gun bullets. The bodies of the Coast Guard personnel were in pretty bad shape, burned and mutilated by the explosions. But at least one man had been shot at close range. The FBI and the Justice Department are investigating the incident. They're still collecting physical evidence.''

"Anything else on the black ship?'' Katz inquired, lighting his cigarette.

"They think they found what was left of it at Collier's Cove,'' Brognola replied. "It was just a burned-out hulk.''

"Does anyone have any idea who these killers are or what they were up to?'' Encizo inquired. "This black ship sounds like a smugglers' vessel to me. Question is, what were they smuggling?''

"Could be a shipment of weaponry to terrorists here in the States,'' McCarter suggested.

"Maybe,'' Brognola replied. "But there's another

possibility. Kurtzman's computer link to the San Francisco Police Department picked up a report about the arrest of a drug dealer. Turned out to be a bigger bust than the narcotics cops expected. Eight pounds of heroin.''

''Eight pounds of horse from a street dealer?'' James whistled softly. ''That much dope could rake in a fortune.''

''And you think the attack on the Coast Guard and the heroin are connected?'' Manning asked Brognola.

''I think there's a strong possibility,'' the Fed replied. ''The pusher squealed like a stuck pig, hoping to make a deal with the cops. He didn't have much to deal with. The guy claimed he got the dope from some mysterious characters who keep a low profile and strict security. They also told him they got a brand new source of heroin. *Lots* of heroin.''

''Oh, shit,'' James muttered. ''Sounds like MERGE is alive and well and peddling dope in Frisco.''

Phoenix Force had clashed with MERGE during their last mission. The Mafia had been crippled by the long Executioner wars. Bolan had killed most of the monarchs of organized crime, and remaining mob members had scattered in all directions.

The surviving factions of organized crime had had three years to recover from their defeat at the hands of Mack Bolan. Some had joined forces to try to revive the Mafia. Some had formed smaller syndicates or even teamed up with certain terrorist groups. But the biggest and most dangerous threat of all was MERGE.

Segments of the Mafia had merged with ambitious portions of other large criminal networks to form a new and fearsome international evil. MERGE had partners in the powerful Corsican syndicate that dominates much of the organized crime in Western Europe. MERGE had allies among the ruthless Mexican mafia, modeled in the image of La Cosa Nostra, and the insidious Colombian syndicate that had become the major force in the cocaine business.

MERGE had quietly formed a secret empire in the shadows. Phoenix Force had discovered the terrible new crime network while trying to solve the assassination of a U.S. congressman in Nassau. They had crushed the MERGE operations in the Bahamas, but the Force realized this was just a small portion of an enormous criminal organization.

"Well," Manning began with a fatalistic shrug, "we knew we hadn't seen the last of MERGE when we left the Bahamas. I guess we just didn't figure we'd run into the bastards again quite so soon."

"Yeah," James agreed. "We stopped about a ton of heroin from being delivered into the hands of MERGE at Freeport. All that horse wasn't just for distribution in the Bahamas. MERGE had planned to ship most of it to the States. The Corsicans couldn't have made another major delivery of dope this quickly."

"Don't bet on it, amigo," Encizo said dryly. "For all we know MERGE might have major caches of heroin all over the United States. I wouldn't underestimate what they're capable of."

"We might not be dealing with MERGE this time," Katz declared. "Remember that mission last year in Turkey? The KGB was supervising the production of heroin for distribution to the West in order to cause unrest and turmoil. Moscow never sleeps, and just because a plan didn't work the first time doesn't mean the Kremlin won't try again."

"Yakov has a point," McCarter agreed. "But whether these blokes are MERGE or KGB, they've bloody well got to be stopped. Especially if they're ruthless enough to slaughter a Coast Guard patrol and shoot down a ruddy helicopter.''

"And whoever did it is almost certainly somewhere in California,'' Brognola added. "Of course, they could have hopped on a plane and flown somewhere else by now, but they must have had something on board that black ship that they were willing to kill for. We figure they'll probably hang around California for a while. They might be involved in the heroin traffic in San Francisco; that's what you guys are going to find out.''

"Well, Frisco is my former stompin' ground,'' James commented. "I can probably still find my way around. Looks like I'll be giving you guys the grand tour of the city.''

"Seems like the logical place to start hunting,'' McCarter said cheerfully, eager to begin the mission.

"You'll have a contact with the Justice Department in San Francisco,'' the Fed explained. "A case officer named Trumball. You've also got a cover for the mission as a special Interpol team. Your identifications with cover names are being processed right now.''

"Any problems with transporting weapons and special equipment?'' Katz inquired.

"That's been taken care of,'' Brognola answered. "And you'll have special federal firearms permits to carry concealed weapons anywhere in the United States. This includes full-auto weapons. Be sure to take anything and everything you figure you might need on this mission because you're going up against a pack of real savages this time.''

"Like I said before,'' Encizo said with a sigh. "What else is new?''

3

A blanket of heavy fog drifted across the San Francisco Bay area. The famous Golden Gate Bridge, the internationally recognized symbol of the city, was a ghostly blur in the gray-shrouded sky.

The warehouse was one of many located along the harbor. It was the property of the Irish Workhorse, a small freight company owned by O'Malley Enterprises. The men would not be disturbed as they conducted their business inside the warehouse storage room. No one would hear the hammering of fists against flesh or the moans of victims. No one except the men involved in the covert "disciplinary action."

Hector Montoya, a Colombian syndicate enforcer, calmly puffed on the black stem of a short cigarette holder as he watched his henchmen punch and kick the three figures cringing helplessly on the floor. The beating was administered with methodical skill. The victims were savagely thrashed by the hoodlums, but their tormentors were careful not to break bones or rupture organs—at least not until they were instructed to take the discipline to the next level.

"*¡Alto!*" Montoya announced when he decided the beating had gone far enough. "We don't want to kill them. Not yet, anyway."

"*Sí, jefe,*" a hoodlum replied as he delivered a final kick to the ribs of one of the victims.

"This is a sad thing for me," Montoya said, tapping

the ash from the end of his cigarette. "After all, we share a similar Spanish heritage, no?"

The three battered victims were pulled into a kneeling position by the thugs. The hapless trio had been bound hand and foot before the beating began. They stared up at Montoya in helpless terror as the ringleader approached.

"We Spanish take pride in the fact we always keep our word," Montoya mused aloud. "But you three have not done so. You promised to pay us the money today."

"Señor Montoya," Ricardo Garcia began, blood oozing from a split lip. "Just give us a couple more days, *por favor*."

"A couple of days?" Montoya replied, raising his black eyebrows in mock horror. "But you told me you'd have the money *today*, Garcia."

"We had trouble raising the money," Garcia said nervously. "It was not as easy as we thought."

"Getting money is never easy, *chico*," Montoya declared as he lowered his cigarette and aimed the burning end at Garcia's face. "But everything in life has a price and if you cannot afford cocaine, you should have kept smoking marijuana and popping pills. You three wanted to sample the rich man's candy and now you must pay for your pleasures."

"We'll get you the money tomorrow," Tomas Lopez, one of Garcia's unfortunate companions said. "Twenty-four hours. Surely that won't make any difference."

"The fate of the world can change in twenty-four hours," Montoya replied as he moved the glowing tip of his cigarette closer to Garcia's face. "Time is important to the people I work for. They will be angry with me if I don't deliver payment. This is why I am angry with you three *cucarachas*. I trusted you to keep your word and you did not. Now you have made a big problem for me.''

"Killing us won't change anything," cried Fernando Santos, the third victim of Montoya's rage.

"I wouldn't have you killed," the Colombian smiled, moving the burning cigarette toward Garcia's left eye. "But I may have to make an example of you three. An example to serve as a warning to others who might think they can cheat me. *¿Comprende?*"

"Cristo," Garcia gasped as he tried to turn his face away from the cigarette. A hoodlum grabbed his hair with one hand and his jaw with the other to hold his head stationary.

"I could burn out your eyeballs and make an example of you that way," Montoya commented. "Maybe I just blind each of you in one eye so you can still go steal the money you owe me."

"Midnight," Garcia whimpered. "We'll have the money for you by midnight."

"All of it?" Montoya demanded. "Every cent you owe me, *chico*?"

"Sí," Garcia confirmed. "One thousand dollars."

"One thousand five hundred," the Colombian corrected. "I'm charging you idiots for making us hunt you down. Our time is valuable. I don't like you messing with our time."

"Five hundred is a lot to ask of these scum, *jefe*," one of the henchmen remarked. "Perhaps you should show some mercy for the retarded."

Montoya laughed. He moved the cigarette away from Garcia's face. The terrified man nearly fainted with relief.

"We'll make it one thousand two hundred and fifty," Montoya decided. "Merciful enough?"

"Sí," Garcia agreed. "We'll have it for you by midnight, Señor Montoya. *Gracias, jefe.*"

"Don't thank me yet," the Colombian warned. "I'll run out of mercy at midnight. If I don't have my money then, I will turn you three into pumpkins—or some sort of sightless vegetable. *¿Comprende?*"

Indeed, the three men understood all too well.

RICARDO GARCIA, Tomas Lopez and Fernando Santos prowled the streets of San Francisco like three desperate animals in search of prey. The trio considered robbing a liquor store, but rejected the idea because it was too dangerous. If only the city ban on handguns had not been declared unconstitutional, Garcia thought glumly. Then three fellows armed only with a knife, a length of chain and a set of homemade knuckle-dusters would not have to be afraid of getting shot when they tried to rob a store.

"We'll just have to get the money in the usual way," Garcia announced wearily.

"But we can't expect to get twelve hundred dollars by stealing purses," Lopez complained. "Not in less than five hours, Ricardo."

"Maybe we should leave town," Santos suggested lamely.

"Montoya would find us," Garcia declared. "Even if we left the state, that Colombian *perro* would catch up with us. We don't have any choice. We'll simply have to mug enough little old ladies to get the money."

The trio selected their stalking ground. They found a dimly lit section of a supermarket parking lot and squatted down by a wire fence, waiting for an easy target to wander in their direction.

An elderly couple hobbled from the supermarket. The old man limped along with a cane while his wife held on to his arm for support as she painfully made her way along. The couple would have been perfect targets if they had only headed toward the area where the three muggers were waiting. Instead, the elderly pair had a kid from the supermarket load their groceries into the trunk of a cab and climbed into the back seat. Garcia and his companions sighed with regret as they watched the taxi disappear from view.

Two men approached their position. Both guys were over six feet tall and built like pro football players with cowboy hats perched on their heads. The pair loaded a case of Coors and some bags of groceries, which probably contained a lot of raw meat and some boxes of shotgun shells, in the back of a Chevy pickup truck. The trio of muggers did not even consider tangling with the two good ol' boys. They were rather relieved when the truck pulled out of the parking lot.

At last, fate seemed to smile on Garcia, Lopez and Santos. Two black women pushed a cart to an old Ford hardtop parked less than six yards from the hoodlums' hiding place. One lady appeared to be about sixty and the other was probably five or six years older. Perfect, Garcia thought. He turned to his *compañeros*. They smiled and nodded in silent agreement.

The trio used tactics as simple and unimaginative as their petty criminal minds. They charged out of the shadows and launched themselves at the startled women. Garcia slammed a boot into the shopping cart and kicked it into one of the women, knocking her to the ground. Lopez grabbed the other woman's purse. She held on to it instinctively.

"Let go, you stupid bitch!" Lopez snarled as he punched her in the face.

Santos rushed to the first woman, who was still on the ground, and kicked her purse out of her hand. It slid across the parking lot. Santos chased after the purse and scooped up his prize.

"Put it down," a voice ordered. "It doesn't go with your outfit."

Santos turned toward the speaker. A man of average height and build gazed back at him. The stranger's complexion was pale, but the folds at the corners of his eyes suggested Mongolian blood mixed with Caucasian. He bent his knees and slowly placed a bag of groceries on the ground.

"What the hell is going on?" Garcia demanded. "We got us a hero here?"

"Maybe a *dead* hero," Lopez sneered, taking a switchblade knife from his pocket. "If he doesn't hand over his wallet."

The stranger calmly reached both hands inside his Windbreaker. The trio stiffened, fearing that the man might have a gun. Then he drew out two narrow objects, each about one foot long. He snapped them open. The stranger was holding two ornate Oriental fans decorated with gold dragon designs above a yin and yang symbol.

"Cristo," Lopez snickered. "This *hombre* is *muy loco!"*

"He's a fuckin' faggot," Garcia spat out with contempt.

"Well, queer boy," Santos began as he slipped a set of wooden knuckle-dusters over the fingers of his right hand. "I'm gonna bust you up!"

He attacked the stranger, feinting a right cross and throwing a fast left jab from the shoulder. The defender raised a fan sharply. It struck Santos's wrist with surprising force. Blood oozed from cut flesh.

Santos swung a right fist at the stranger's head as hard as he could. The man snapped a fan shut and chopped it across Santos's wrist. He then slashed the other fan to the side of the mugger's skull. Santos staggered from the blow, amazed and stunned by how hard the fan struck.

The stranger quickly stabbed the end of a closed fan into Santos's solar plexus. The hood doubled up with a choking gasp. His opponent bent a knee and slammed it under Santos's jaw. Teeth crunched and broke at their roots, and Fernando Santos collapsed to the ground with barely a whimper.

"*¡Que la chigada!*" Lopez snarled as he pressed the button of his knife. A five-inch blade snapped into place. "I'm gonna cut your balls off!"

The stranger noticed that Lopez held the knife like a novice, but he did not underestimate his opponent. Even a clod can be dangerous, and even the best trained expert can make a mistake. One tiny error is enough to get one killed in a life-and-death struggle.

He danced away from the first knife slash and parried a thrust with the fan in his right hand. Lopez suddenly slashed his blade at the other fan, planning to cut it in half. The fan moved abruptly and the knife whistled through the air.

The stranger quickly swung the fan in his right hand. The steel ribs of the innocent-looking instrument struck the knife, ripping it from Lopez's grasp. The mugger cried out, startled to discover his hand was bleeding. The stranger whirled and slashed his other fan across the hood's face. Lopez shrieked and stumbled backward. His left cheek had been sliced open from the eyelid to the corner of his mouth.

"*Madre de Dios,*" Ricardo Garcia gasped, horrified by what he had just witnessed.

Garcia removed a three-foot-long motorcycle chain from his waist, but it was already too late to come to the rescue of Tomas Lopez. The stranger had flapped the fans in a rapid gesture to distract and disorient Lopez.

Then he kicked the mugger squarely in the balls. Lopez folded up, clutching his mashed testicles and vomiting on the asphalt. His opponent stepped forward and closed a fan, chopping its steel rim into the mastoid behind Lopez's right ear. The hood fell unconscious, landing face first in his own vomit.

Ricardo Garcia attacked swiftly, hoping to catch the formidable stranger off guard. The chain lashed out at the man's face, but a fan rose to block the attack. Steel links slashed the cloth between the sturdy ribs of the fan, but the stranger whipped his other fan into the chain and trapped it.

Garcia pulled hard, trying to free his weapon. The stranger did not resist and leaped forward to launch a vicious side kick to Garcia's midsection. The mugger fell as if his stomach had exploded.

The stranger hammered the butt of a steel fan into the ulna nerve in Garcia's right arm, and the chain slipped from trembling fingers. Before Garcia could react, the stranger chopped him across the corner of the jaw. Garcia was already losing consciousness when a roundhouse kick to the head knocked him out cold.

"I seen it," one of the ladies whispered as she helped her friend get up. "But I ain't sure I believe it."

HECTOR MONTOYA PLACED A VALISE on his lap and opened it as he rode in the back seat of a pearl-gray Mercedes. The Colombian counted the number of plastic packets containing cocaine. Twenty-two left. Enough to take care of the customers he had to see that night, with five or six packs left for his own personal use.

"Hey, *jefe*," said Ramon Chavez, a Mexican Mafia goon who had been assigned to assist Montoya. "We gonna party tonight, man?"

"Maybe," Montoya replied. "We still got some deals to take care of first. Don't forget about Garcia and those other two idiots."

"They won't come up with the money," Pedro Morales, the driver, muttered. "They aren't good enough thieves to steal that much cash in five hours."

"Then we'll just have to take whatever they've got," Montoya said with a shrug. "Including their lives, eh?"

The henchmen laughed as the Mercedes approached a traffic light at the intersection of Taraval Street and Nineteenth Avenue. Morales stopped the car for a red light. He always obeyed traffic laws, especially when he was carrying cocaine.

"You know," Chavez began, "I always figured only rich people used cocaine, but you've got a lot of coke customers in the lower-middle classes."

"The supply increased when MERGE took over," Montoya explained. "We could lower the prices to meet the demand for cocaine among lower-income people. Profits have increased, and cocaine is more popular than ever."

"Nice to be part of the American free-enterprise system," Chavez said, chuckling.

None of the gangsters paid any attention to the young Oriental who pedaled up to the Mercedes on a bicycle. The man leaned forward and placed a gray metal disc against the trunk of the car. Then he steered his bike onto the sidewalk and pedaled around the edge of a building. Montoya noticed the Oriental just before he disappeared around the corner.

"Don't know why they let those people into the country," he said sourly.

"Who do you mean?" Chavez asked.

"Vietnamese," the Colombian replied with a shrug.

"Laotians, Cambodians and all the rest. I hate those yellow slants. Don't trust them. They're sneaky."

"Sí," Morales said with a smile. "Not honest and trustworthy like us."

The light changed to green, and just as the Mercedes pulled forward the limpet mine exploded, igniting the gas tank and blasting the big car into jagged shards of charred metal. The explosion also smashed the front end of the vehicle behind the Mercedes. The latch to the hood snapped, and the crinkled metal lid was broken off at the hinges. The engine exploded and the windshield shattered, sending a storm of glass into the driver's face and chest.

Burning wreckage littered the street. Screams were heard, and people darted about in fear for their lives. A block away, a man observed the chaos from the fifth floor of a hotel window. He lowered his binoculars and smiled with satisfaction.

"Han hau," the man whispered. "Very good."

4

"Hello, gentlemen," a stocky red-haired man with a bushy mustache said in greeting. "I'm Alex Trumball, Special Investigator for the Department of Justice, Task Force Against Organized Crime."

"Pleasure to meet you," Yakov Katzenelenbogen replied as he showed Trumball his forged identification card. "Gaston Poire, Sûreté, French Interpol."

"You speak English very well, Monsieur Poire," Trumball remarked.

"He speaks six languages fluently," David McCarter told the Department of Justice agent. "Personally, I'm still working on English."

"And you're...?" Trumball began.

"Richard Marlowe," McCarter replied. "British Interpol, Scotland Yard."

"Well, I was told to expect an international group," Trumball commented.

"The rest of the team are Americans," Gary Manning declared. The Canadian's nondescript accent would not betray his true nationality. "I'm Bob Curtis, Interpol Section of the Department of Justice. Special Agents Marshall and Vasquez are checking into a possible lead right now."

"Maybe you guys know something I don't," Trumball stated as he slumped into a chair behind his desk. "I sure hope so, anyway."

"We arrived in San Francisco less than an hour ago,"

McCarter said. "Don't expect too much from us too soon, mate. We're good, but we're not clairvoyant."

"Well, you sure picked one hell of a night to get here," the Justice man said. "Have you had a chance to listen to a radio yet? Somebody set off a car bomb and blew a Mercedes to hell. The Frisco cops are still trying to scrape up evidence off the sidewalk, but they're pretty sure the targets were dope dealers. Of course, some innocent bystanders got killed, too."

"These guys were pushing heroin?" Manning asked.

"The cops think the pushers were with the Colombian syndicate," Trumball answered. "So it was probably cocaine."

"Any suspicions concerning who hit them or why?" Katz asked, sinking into a chair in front of Trumball's desk.

"Not yet," Trumball said with a shrug. "Hey, I got one cheery report tonight. Three junkies tried to mug a couple of little old ladies. Then this guy showed up. I think his name is John Trent. Anyway, Trent is some sort of karate expert. He kicked the shit out of those punks."

"I hope nobody charges him for using excessive force or some such nonsense," McCarter remarked, ever the cynic.

"Not very likely that'll happen," Trumball assured him. "Apparently the muggers were armed with chains and knives. This Trent guy must be pretty good at that Jap fighting."

"Indeed," Katz agreed. "But I'm afraid it has no connection with our mission, Mr. Trumball."

"What exactly is your mission?" the Justice man inquired. "I know this is a hush-hush deal, but I'm still on your side, so I'd like to know anything you can tell me."

"Sûreté and Scotland Yard are concerned about the

heroin traffic in America because we believe the Corsican syndicate might be involved," the Israeli explained. "And if they are shipping more drugs to the United States, we can expect to see an increase of narcotics in France and Britain, as well."

"Hope we can help each other," Trumball began. "But all I know is the Frisco narcs busted a low-life named Peterson. The guy has always been a small-time operator, but he had a shit-load of heroin on him that day."

"Did he say where he got it?" Manning asked.

"Peterson came up with one of the champion bullshit stories of all time," Trumball replied. "The little turd claims he was kidnapped from whatever rock he lives under. He expects us to believe he was handcuffed and blindfolded by somebody who stuffed him in the back seat of a car. Then he was taken to a dimly lit room where he was asked if he'd like to become a big-time dope pusher with big money. The guys who made the offer always stayed in the shadows so he couldn't see their faces. He also says they spoke through some kind of electronic handkerchief that distorted their voices."

"Sounds pretty farfetched," Katz agreed. "But I wouldn't totally dismiss his story. The improbable is occasionally the truth."

"Hell," Trumball said, clucking his tongue. "I can tell you where the heroin must have come from. That much horse has to be from the personal stables of Ian O'Malley. I'd bet my reputation, my paycheck and my old lady's ass on that."

"Ian O'Malley," Manning said with a frown. "The name sounds vaguely familiar."

"O'Malley was under investigation a few years ago after the Executioner busted up the Mafia operations in Frisco," Trumball explained. "O'Malley didn't take the fall, but there's no doubt that he was connected with the mob. He still is. Apparently he got promoted to honorary *capo*. O'Malley's now known as the Irish don."

"Then the Mafia is still active in San Francisco?" Katz asked.

"Since Mack Bolan's been gone," Trumball stated. "Nobody is quite sure who runs the organized crime scene anymore, but O'Malley is involved in it up to his neck. Of course, what we know and what we can prove are two different things."

"Well," McCarter began with a grin, "maybe we can do something about this Irish don. What else have you learned about that incident with the Coast Guard patrol boat and the black ship?"

"Not much," the Justice agent confessed. "But one interesting fact popped up. Bullets taken from one of the dead men were sent to the FBI forensic department. The .45 slugs were from a regular 1911A1 Colt pistol. The killers probably took it from a dead Guardsman. But there were also a number of 9mm parabellum slugs recovered from the bodies."

"That's an international cartridge," Manning commented. "The parabellum round is used all over the world."

"Yeah." Trumball nodded. "But ballistics and metal composition suggest it was fired from a Japanese Type 57 Nambu pistol. Now, if that isn't weird enough, they also think the weapon used to shoot down the chopper was probably a .30-caliber Type 41 light machine gun."

"Chinese version of the Canadian Mark Two Bren gun," McCarter commented. "Saw a few of them when I was stationed in Hong Kong a few years ago."

"So the black ship may have come from the Orient," Katz mused. "That is interesting, although it doesn't answer any questions. Just adds one more to the list."

"Any ideas about finding some answers?" Trumball asked, holding his hands palms up in a hopeless gesture.

"I'm sure we'll come up with something," the unit commander of Phoenix Force assured him. "We always get results."

5

The Grand Opening was a flashy nightclub on Mission Street. The atmosphere was quasi-disco with pulsating lights, plastic furniture and rock bands that played music loud enough to bury whatever words there might be to their songs. Of course, the success of a lead singer seems to depend more on how well he or she can move about dressed in tight clothing than what his or her voice is like.

The Grand Opening attracted people from all levels of society, and all of them were looking for action of one kind or another. Hookers and pimps were regular customers, hustling for tricks and watching out for vice cops. Studs on the make, dope peddlers selling everything from pills to heroin, fences dealing in hot merchandise and other assorted nightlife devotees could be found at the Grand Opening. Gays generally avoided the place because several homosexuals had been beaten and robbed at the club. One victim died from internal bleeding.

Calvin James and Rafael Encizo entered the Grand Opening and began shuffling through the crowded nightclub. The black commando was familiar with the place. He had advised Encizo to wear casual clothing and foot gear.

"No black dress shoes whatever you do," James warned. "Around here that's the same as wearing a sign that says you're either a cop, a soldier or a priest.

Nobody's gonna figure either of us for a priest, and we're a little older than most soldiers. That leaves cop. The club will empty out so fast it'll look like a fire drill. And watch your wallet. Some light-fingered dudes hang out at the Grand Opening.''

The Phoenix Force pair did not draw unwanted attention as they moved through the nightclub. James wore a wide-brimmed hat and a white jacket with matching designer jeans. His shirt was open to the navel, and two gold chains hung from his neck. Although the place was dark, James wore sunglasses. He looked more like a pimp than a commando. That was the idea.

Encizo had selected a Levi's jacket and slacks. He followed his partner's example and donned a pair of dark glasses before entering the club. The Cuban hoped James knew what he was doing. Inside, he discovered his concern was needless. More than half the customers of the Grand Opening wore dark glasses.

"Looks like a pink-eye epidemic," Encizo remarked.

"Lot of bashful folks here," James told him. "They don't want anyone to get a good look at their faces. Some of them are covering up their eyes because the pupils are dilated owing to recreational use of controlled substances that has gotten out of control. In other words, they're spaced-out junkies."

The pair cut their way along the bar as a few dozen figures danced and contorted to the throbbing rhythm of the noisy rock band. The lead singer shouted repetitious words into a microphone as he punched a spike-studded fist into the air. The dancers jerked their bodies to the motion, as if they were puppets responding to a sharp pull on their strings.

"Maybe I'm getting old," the Cuban muttered.

"What's that?" James asked, unable to hear his partner over the loud music.

"Nothing important," Encizo replied. "Have you found your friend yet?"

"Not yet," James answered. "But this is one of his favorite haunts."

"He mustn't have much respect for his eardrums," Encizo commented dryly.

"The dude doesn't have much respect for anything," James declared. "And speak of the devil, there he is."

James led Encizo to a booth at a corner of the room. A scrawny little black man sat at the table, talking to a pair of white girls who did not look old enough to legally enter the Grand Opening. The dude glanced up at James and crinkled his brow as if he had just suffered a terrible headache.

"My main man, Leon." James smiled as he slid into the seat next to the little hustler. "Long time no see, eh, Leon?"

"Not long enough," Leon whispered through his teeth as he forced a smile.

"These sweet young things for us, Leon?" James inquired as he leaned toward the girls. They shuddered as he licked his lips. "Break 'em in on the S&M routine yet, man?"

"Uh...we gotta go," one of the girls said nervously. "Catch you later, Leon."

The girls hurried from the booth, and Encizo took the vacant seat across from Leon and James. The hustler squirmed like a rabbit in a trap.

"That was some cold shit you pulled on me, Cal," Leon sniveled. "I don't have my girls do no S&M, man."

"Give them a break, Leon," James replied. "Let the girls finish junior high before you try to recruit them. Wouldn't want to have to haul your ass in for corrupting the morals of a minor."

"I ain't corruptin' nobody," Leon said with a pout.

"Oh, yeah?" James chuckled. "Hey, you still poppin' pills, Leon?"

The black warrior turned to Encizo.

"See, Leon is a jack-of-all-trades," he explained. "Hookers, dope, black-market merchandise and small-scale fencing, little Leon does it all. Trouble is, our boy here gets too fond of the stuff he deals in so he uses it himself, too. Never make big time or big money that way, Leon. Bet you've got a pocketful of uppers and downers on you. Black beauties, red devils, quaaludes. What you got, my man?"

"I ain't got shit," Leon told him. "Besides, I thought you wasn't a cop no more, Cal. You left Frisco more than a year ago, man. What you tryin' to shake me down for? Gone into business for yourself, Cal?"

"Never mind what I'm doing these days," James replied. "All you need to know is I can still bust you. I still have connections on the force, Leon. I got connections you don't want to fuck with, man. You'd better believe that, Leon. I can have your ass in the state pen within forty-eight hours. They'll burn you for parole violation if nothing else, bro."

"Okay." Leon frowned. "What do you want from me, man?"

"Information," James answered. "Same as always. You were always an A-number-one informer, Leon. We want you to be a canary and do a little singing for us."

"Us?" Leon said, glancing at Encizo. "Who's this dude?"

"Pancho Villa," the Cuban said grimly. "And if you don't cooperate, we'll take you outside and do a little Mexican hat dance on your head, punk."

"Ease up, man," James urged. "Leon is gonna talk to us. Right, Leon?"

"Shit." The hustler frowned. "What you want to know?"

"Word has it there's a lot of horse on the streets these days, Leon," James said. "We want to know where it's coming from."

"I don't do no horse," Leon declared. "Don't use it, don't sell it, don't fuck with no needles. You know that, Cal."

"Yeah," James said as he nodded. "But you know people who do. What about Freddy?"

"Freddy Jackson?" Leon said. "Man, you been outta town too long. Freddy don't deal heroin no more. He dipped his hand into the collection plate one time too many. The Irishman didn't like that. So Freddy wound up committin' suicide. Took a swan dive off a tall building. Death by natural causes, man."

"The Irishman?" Encizo asked.

"You boys are really from outta town," Leon replied with a snort. "O'Malley is the dude. Ian O'Malley. He's Mister Mafia in San Francisco. Don't ask me why the wops let an Irishman run the show. Maybe he's all they have left after the Executioner did a number on the mob, but O'Malley is *the Man* now."

"O'Malley is dealing the heroin?" James asked.

"I can't say for sure." Leon smiled. "Seems I got a mental block. Also seems like I'm givin' you valuable information for nothin', man. Shit. What kinda businessman you think I am?"

"The kind who will get three hundred bucks if he keeps talking," James replied. "And his ass kicked if he doesn't."

"Stay cool, man," Leon urged. "Stay cool. I can't say for sure about the heroin. O'Malley has been working with the spics lately...."

He turned fearfully toward Encizo. The Cuban glared at him.

"No offense, man," Leon said. "I mean the Mexican Mafia and those Colombian dudes in the cocaine business. Coke is big, you know. Besides, the horse supply had dried up until just a couple of days ago."

"You haven't earned three hundred bucks yet, Leon," James warned. "Cheaper for us to just kick your ass."

"Wait a minute," the hustler insisted. "Now, a friend of mine named Phil deals some horse. He tells me that he was sort of kidnapped right off the fuckin' street by a couple of chinks. Maybe they were Japs or Vietnamese or somethin'. Anyway, they take Phil to a car. Blindfold him and drive all over town before they haul his ass into a room where these dudes are hidin' in the shadows and talkin' to him through one of those boxes that makes your voice sound like a robot in one of those sci-fi movies."

"Bullshit," Encizo growled. "Let's kick this guy's ass until he's wearing it on his neck."

"Hey, I ain't bullshittin' you," Leon insisted. "And Phil ain't the imaginative type. Anyway, they gave Phil a caseful of heroin and a bunch of cash as a down payment. They told him he'd be workin' for them from now on. Promised the dude a bigger cut than he got before. Phil asked how they could do business if he didn't know who they were. They told him not to worry about that. They'd find him when they wanted him. Phil asked what if the Irishman sends somebody for him. The chinks said they'd take care of that, too."

"Okay, Leon," James said as he opened his wallet. "Here's your bread. If you're lying about any of this, we'll catch up with you sooner or later."

"You know me—" Leon smiled "—my information is always good, man. That's three hundred, right?"

"Just pay him two hundred," Encizo declared. "I didn't like him using the term 'spic.' That's going to cost him one way or the other."

"Hey, man," Leon whined. "I didn't mean nothin' personal. Why don't you just call me a nigger and that'll make us even?"

"One hundred bucks," Encizo said firmly. "Or I break your arm."

"Shit." Leon pouted. "Okay, I'll settle for two hundred."

"Cheer up, Leon," James said. "You made a profit and got a valuable lesson on race relations. Maybe you'll be a social worker someday."

"Sure wish you hadn't run off those girls," Leon said regretfully. "Hard to get fresh talent these days."

"From now on recruit twenty-one or older," James warned. "I don't want to hear that you're robbing cradles, Leon. That could get your ass in jail, my man."

"If you're lucky," Encizo added with an edge in his voice. "Let's get some fresh air, Cal."

The Phoenix Force pair left the Grand Opening and headed for their rented Toyota in the parking lot. Four white guys dressed in mail-order cowboy outfits followed them outside. James glanced over his shoulder and noticed one of the red-necks knelt to pull a bowie knife from his boot.

"We've got company," the black man whispered to Encizo.

"I know," Encizo replied softly. "How many?"

"Two for you and two for me," James answered, opening his jacket.

"You boys goin' somewhere?" a man with a Texas drawl demanded.

"Gotta go home and get some sleep," Encizo replied. "Got a big day of lettuce picking to do tomorrow."

"That's real cute, greaser." A beefy cowboy chuckled as he slid a belt from his thick waist. The heavy buckle was made of brass and already dented from previous use. "But you and the nigger got a lot of cash on you already."

"How many welfare checks you boys pick up each week?" another red-neck snorted as he raised a six-inch bowie. "Bet you boys use about a dozen different names and shuffle all over the state to different welfare offices, don't you?"

"We seen you give a lot of money to that other nigger inside," a bearded punk with a .22-caliber High-Standard derringer in his fist declared. "But you're gonna give the rest of your cash to us, right?"

"I'll tell you what I'll give you," James began as he turned to point a Colt Commander at the bearded man's stomach. "I'll give you a .45-caliber navel if you don't drop that peashooter right now."

"Oh, Christ," the guy gasped, dropping his derringer.

Encizo had drawn a Walther PPK from shoulder leather and aimed it at the man with the knife. The bowie fell to the ground, and the guy raised his hands. The others followed his example.

"We'd love to kick your dumb asses all over this parking lot," James announced. "But we don't have time for that. Just step away from your hardware and keep your hands up."

Encizo kept his pistol trained on the four troublemakers while James moved forward to confiscate the weapons. The bearded punk suddenly yanked off his Stetson and grabbed another .22 derringer from his hat.

The Cuban's PPK cracked, a tongue of flame jetting from its barrel. A .380 hollowpoint projectile ripped into the red-neck's upper arm, tearing biceps. Then the bullet struck bone and expanded on contact. The hood screamed as the derringer fell from his hand. He slumped to his knees, clutching his bullet-smashed limb. His eyes rolled upward, and he passed out with a sigh that sounded almost relieved.

The big dude made a wild lunge for Calvin James, hoping to catch the black man off guard. James easily dodged the clumsy attack and batted the steel frame of his Colt pistol across the guy's right elbow. The assailant yelped in pain. James shuffled behind the man and pumped a foot into his rump to send him hurtling into the rear of a Dodge pickup.

Another country-fried moron launched himself at James, and the black enforcer blocked a punch with his forearm and rammed the muzzle of his Commander into the man's gut. James hooked his left fist to the guy's jaw and slashed a karate chop under his opponent's sternum. He then whipped a backfist to the jerk's temple and the cowboy fell unconscious at James's feet.

The big red-neck bellowed like a bull with a hot coal up its ass. He lunged once more, hoping to attack James from behind. The black warrior pivoted and launched a high side kick. The bottom of his foot slammed into the yahoo's face, and the big man staggered backward from the kick, blood oozing from his crushed nose. James quickly moved in and backhanded the barrel of his Colt across the goon's jaw. The cowboy fell against the pickup and slumped into dreamland.

The last red-neck who was still on his feet proved to be as dumb as his companions. With a rebel yell he charged Encizo, planning to wrench the Walther from the Cuban's grasp. The tactic almost worked because Encizo was slightly distracted by James's fight with the other two drugstore cowboys.

The Cuban turned in time to see the last yahoo leap

forward. He could have shot the bastard but held his fire, reluctant to shoot an unarmed opponent who posed only a minimal threat. Encizo suddenly ducked under the guy's groping arms and rammed a shoulder into his belly.

Encizo scooped up the cowboy's legs and stood abruptly, lifting the guy over his back. The red-neck turned head over heels and crashed to the ground. Encizo kicked the guy in the side of the head, the steel toe of his boot striking just above the vulnerable temple to render the man unconscious.

"I reckon that wraps up the O.K. Corral Part Two," Calvin James remarked as he shoved his .45 into its holster. "You okay, pard?"

"Fine," Encizo assured him. "Let's get out of here before somebody calls the police."

"Nobody at the Grand Opening is likely to call the cops," James said with a shrug. "Nobody inside that joint would have heard anything and nobody outside would have seen anything. They're real good at looking the other way when stuff like this happens."

"Humor me," Encizo urged. "Let's get the hell out of here."

6

Harold Kuming and Andrew Tanaka rode the elevator to the fourteenth floor of the Willow Inn Hotel on Geary Boulevard. They did not speak. Two steel balls clicked methodically as Kuming's fingers worked them around and around in his hand.

The balls were used to strengthen his fingers. The muscular Chinese American was an expert in Cantonese *chuan fa*, which most Westerners incorrectly refer to as kung fu. Harold Kuming specialized in the tiger-claw technique. He could literally tear a man apart with his bare hands, and he had done so on more than one occasion.

A keen-eyed observer might have noticed the tattoo of a forked tongue at the inside of Kuming's wrist. A black serpent was etched into the man's flesh, concealed by the sleeve of his suit jacket. The tattoo was the emblem of the Yi-chyun Hai Shee—the Black Serpent Society.

Andrew Tanaka was an athletic man, smaller and less muscular than Kuming, but very quick and agile as a cat. He sported a small Hitler-style mustache and wore his hair in bangs to further exhibit his bad taste. Tanaka was also a practitioner of martial arts, skilled in karate, *ken-jutsu* and *masaki-ryu*—the use of a weighted chain called a *manrikigusari*. Roughly two and one-half feet long, the chain was folded in half and carried in his belt beneath his jacket.

The Japanese American also bore a snake tattoo beneath his Western business suit. Tanaka's skin was adorned with numerous colorful designs and pictures. Lotus flowers, cherry blossoms and bamboo stalks had been drawn across his back and chest. The largest tattoo was a fierce green serpent extending from his buttocks to his shoulder blades. The reptile's open jaws revealed white fangs and a scarlet forked tongue.

Tanaka, however, was not a member of the Black Serpent Society. He belonged to the Hebi Uji—the Snake Clan. The two organizations had more in common than the same reptilian symbol. Both the Serpent Society and the Snake Clan had begun centuries ago in the Orient. Both organizations were devoted to the same sinister business—international crime.

The Black Serpent Society was a Chinese tong. Originally formed in 1646, the tong secret societies combated the Manchu tyranny that had flooded throughout China. However, the tong lacked the organization and manpower of the White Lotus Society, which had helped defeat the Mongol rule in China and establish the Ming Dynasty in 1368. To finance the new revolution, the tong societies turned to a variety of unsavory ventures, including the opium trade, white slavery and murderers for hire.

Perhaps this "the end justifies the means" philosophy had once been a sincere effort to free China of the yoke of Manchu rule, but the tong discovered a new form of power and wealth in organized crime. Members became more interested in profits from gambling houses, brothels and opium dens than patriotism. When Chinese began to emigrate to the countries of the West, the tong societies extended to new horizons.

The Black Serpent Society became one of the few truly international tong networks. With branches in the

United States and Western Europe, its influence was more widespread than any tong except the Brothers of Heaven and Earth, better known as the Triad.

The Black Serpent tong operated criminal syndicates in America long before the Mafia, having first gotten a foothold in San Francisco's Chinatown in the early 1850s. The area had been a hotbed of tong activity in those days, and fierce competition among the various societies led to full-scale tong wars. Hatchet-wielding killers roamed the streets of San Francisco and, it is said, blood flowed like small rivers in the gutters. The war ended in 1860 when the tong negotiated terms for a truce and the "Five Companies" were formed, almost a century before the Mafia established their "Five Families."

The Companies, named after the five provinces of China, were the elite ruling class of tong activities in San Francisco. The smaller sects were either absorbed by the Companies or exterminated during the tong wars. The Black Serpent Society was one of the Five Companies. Tong operations continued to flourish in the United States although they kept a low profile and seldom carried out business beyond the confines of Chinese districts.

Harold Kuming's father had been a member of the Black Serpent tong and his father before him. The Kuming family was proud of this heritage. They believed the tong had fought tyranny in China, bigotry in America and provided prosperous business opportunities unavailable to most Chinese Americans. Harold Kuming was proud and honored to wear the Black Serpent tattoo, which he regarded as a family crest.

The history of the Hebi Uji was quite similar. The Snake Clan was a yakuza outfit, with its roots in feudal Japan where the yakuza had been known as "thieves with honor." Unlike the samurai, the yakuza were not knight warriors of noble birth. They were products of the lower classes, yet they learned swordsmanship and other martial arts from *ronin*, renegade mercenary samurai. The yakuza earned a reputation as Robin Hood-style champions of the poor. Some cynics believed the yakuza only helped the peasant classes in order to gain their cooperation, but there can be no doubt that yakuza swordsmen bravely fought brutal gangs of bandits and pillaging samurai on more than one occasion. The villages they protected regarded the yakuza as heroes, regardless of what their motives might have been.

Despite virtuous origins, the yakuza, like the tong, became more concerned with profit than defending the oppressed. The clans became criminal organizations, dealing in gambling, prostitution and gunrunning. Narcotics is not as lucrative in Japan as it is in the Western countries or most of the Orient, but a few yakuza did get into the dope business. Most *obyan* clan leaders considered the market dishonorable and refused to participate in narcotics.

Many of the old "Mustache Pete" mafiosi had felt the same way about drugs in the 1940s, although supply and demand and competition among the Five Families pressured unwilling mobsters to join the dope race. Such pressures did not exist in Japan and the yakuza were reluctant to extend business beyond their homeland. However, a few ambitious *obyan* dared to escalate operations to the United States after World War II.

The yakuza were new to America. The Mafia and the tong had already established crime networks in the U.S. that were far larger than the Japanese could hope to match. The Spanish syndicates and black gangster groups were also growing, and the yakuza seemed powerless to compete against the established forces of organized crime in America.

Then came the new age of industrial growth in Japan. Tokyo-based businesses were involved in everything from steel and automobiles to digital watches and video-tapes. American corporations eagerly made deals with the Japanese. Some of these businesses were actually owned and operated by yakuza *obyan* leaders. Capitalism had come to Japan and the ancient order of "honorable thieves" were ready for it.

The Hebi Uji was one of the most powerful and largest of the yakuza clans. It had already established a foothold in America and it wisely recruited Japanese Americans in order to operate efficiently in a Western culture. When Japan suddenly joined the giants of international trade, the Snake Clan received the financial support and business connections needed to become a power within the United States.

Despite having similar criminal interests, some Japanese regard the Chinese with contempt, and some Chinese still feel resentment and antagonism toward the Japanese. Thus the tong and the yakuza were rivals, competitors in the business of crime. Five years ago, Harold Kuming and Andrew Tanaka would not have entered an elevator together unless one of them planned to kill the other. They would never be friends or trust each other as they did the members of their own sect. Yet circumstances had made the Black Serpent Society and the Snake Clan allies. They were now partners and united for the sake of a common cause under the banner of a new organization known as TRIO.

The elevator doors opened on the fourteenth floor. Kuming and Tanaka stepped into the corridor, and two stern-faced Orientals met them at the entrance. The men wore pistols in shoulder holsters beneath their suit jackets.

"Ana'ta no o-nama wah, dozo?" one of the sentries inquired.

He wanted to know their names. Tanaka answered.

"Tanaka Andro," the Japanese American replied with a bow. *"Kuming-san oh-go-shokai."*

"Konnichi-wah," the sentry replied as he bowed in return. *"Ee-kaga desu kah?"*

The guard had asked, "How are you?" This was not an idle question, but part of a password that had been arranged.

"Kono-ha ga itami-masu," Tanaka answered, claiming he had a toothache.

"O torimas, dozo," the sentry said, smiling as he stepped aside.

Tanaka and Kuming moved through the corridor. More guards patrolled the area. All were Oriental and armed with a variety of handguns and compact machine pistols. Sentries asked for permission to search the pair for weapons and hidden microphones. The request was polite, but Kuming and Tanaka realized they could not refuse to be frisked. They surrendered their pistols without protest. The *manrikigusari* fighting chain and steel balls were also confiscated.

The guards expertly frisked them, checking for concealed weapons at their ankles, wrists and the napes of their necks. Satisfied, the sentries escorted them to a door. Kuming and Tanaka removed their shoes before they entered the penthouse apartment, and as soon as they crossed the threshold, they felt as if they had entered a time machine and stepped into a different era.

Oriental tapestries covered the walls, and illustrated the magnificent Gate of Edo, the Great Wall of China and fierce Mongol horsemen led by Genghis Khan in brilliant color and superb artistry. Jasmine incense burned from the ornate brass jaws of dragon and serpent statues.

Kuming and Tanaka bowed deeply to three figures seated on a raised platform at the opposite end of the room. They resembled a trio of Oriental emperors, which, in a very real sense, was exactly what they were.

Wang Tse-Tu, the *ling shyou*, or leader, of the Black Serpent tong sat on a great throne. His hands were curled over the armrests, and each of his fingernails was at least four inches long. Wang was an incredible figure, dressed in a green *mang-p'ao* dragon robe with a long purple *p'u fu* jacket. A decorative *ling t'ou* court collar flared from his shoulders like the roof of a pagoda.

An obese man, Wang filled the oversize chair. A court cap with a peacock-feather tassel was mounted on his head. Wang's eyes were knife slits in a smooth round face. A stringy gray beard and mandarin mustache framed his small bowlike mouth. An ornate, square-shaped *pu fang* coat of arms hung from Wang's neck. The symbol of a black three-headed snake against a gold background dominated the amulet.

Shimo Goro sat on the throne beside the tong leader. The middle-aged Japanese was the *obyan* of the infamous Snake Clan of the yakuza. He was an athletic man with powerful shoulders and a thick chest, his muscles honed by many years of *ken-jutsu* sword-fighting and other martial arts. Shimo wore a black kimono and *hakama* culottes. An ornate gold *obi* sash was bound around his waist and held a blue-and-green fan.

A *katana*, the long sword of the samurai, leaned against the armrest of Shimo's throne, and his left hand never wandered far from the hilt of the sword. The *katana* had been crafted by Hashigo Naifu, one of the finest sword makers of the thirteenth century. It had once been the personal weapon of Shimo Karada, a great samurai warrior. Karada had become a *ronin* renegade and later a yakuza. The *katana* and the tradition of leadership of yakuza became the legacy of the Shimo family. Shimo Goro had inherited his position as *obyan* of the Snake Clan. He regarded it as a sacred trust and an honored duty.

Shimo's face was lean and his iron-gray hair was clipped short. His eyes resembled black almonds, and the brows were thick and bushy. Shimo also wore a medallion that bore the likeness of the three-headed serpent.

The third man on the platform was Tosha Khan, a dark man with a fierce face accented by a drooping black mustache streaked with silver. His robe was blood red and fringed with gold. A brass helmet with hornlike decorations was strapped to his head. Chain-mail bracelets were bound to each wrist and forearm. A three-headed snake amulet hung from his neck to rest against the metal breastplate on his chest.

Tosha Khan claimed to be descended from the great Genghis Khan, the Mongol conqueror who united the fierce Mongol tribes and led the Golden Horde to victory after victory. Genghis Khan claimed an empire greater than Alexander's or the Caesars'. The Mongols conquered China, Russia and most of eastern Europe. For two hundred years the Mongolian empire was the most powerful force on the face of the earth.

But the days of glory were gone and the empire of Genghis Khan was only a memory in the minds of historians. The Mongolian People's Republic was now only an extension of the Soviet Union, subject to the tyranny of the Communist leaders in Moscow. The Russians had never forgiven the Golden Horde, and the Kremlin ruled Mongolia with a harsh, often cruel, hand.

Tosha Khan had been born Altajin Illyvich Dzadgad in the Mongolian capital of Ulan Bator. He was descended of the Tartars, and according to the legend of his family, a distant relative had been a favored concubine of Genghis Khan. Young Altajin became obsessed with his alleged heritage. He hated the Communists, who he felt denied him his legacy as an emperor by birthright.

So Tosha Khan, as he came to be known, created a new empire, an empire of crime. He called his network of dope dealers, counterfeiters, white slavers, professional thieves and hired assassins the New Horde. Tosha had traveled throughout the world and recruited his people from all levels of society. Most of the New Horde were Orientals or Eurasians of Mongolian descent. Tosha's shadow empire had branches throughout Asia and parts of eastern Europe, Turkey and even the Soviet Union. The New Horde also conducted smaller operations in France, Spain and Italy.

Tosha Khan had spent almost forty years building the New Horde. It had a wide sphere of activities and considerable manpower, but it still lacked the wealth, influence and well-placed connections of the tong and the yakuza. Thus, Tosha Khan agreed to join forces with his former rivals to create TRIO.

This merger of three great criminal networks made TRIO the most powerful organization of its kind in the Orient. It was even more powerful than the mighty Triad, which had nearly monopolized the opium markets in the Far East until TRIO entered the international narcotics business. Wang, Shimo and Tosha Khan were the absolute rulers of this brilliant and ruthless brotherhood.

"Welcome, Mr. Kuming and Mr. Tanaka," Wang Tse-Tu greeted. "Please come forward and tell us of your progress."

Kuming and Tanaka humbly approached and knelt

before the three emperors. To many Westerners the elaborate props and costumes used by the leaders of TRIO might have seemed absurd. Yet TRIO realized the importance of rituals and ceremony. All things held with reverence are conducted with ritual and ceremony. Religions, military activities, courtrooms and business meetings all have their own procedures, all use props to create a certain desired atmosphere and all demand costumes or uniforms.

Wang and Shimo were pleased that Harold Kuming and Andrew Tanaka observed the rites of their organization. The Oriental Americans displayed great respect and excellent manners as they faced the leaders of TRIO. The Western culture had not corrupted Kuming and Tanaka. Their allegiance was to the three-headed serpent, not the Stars and Stripes.

Tosha Khan felt mixed emotions about the two Oriental Americans. The Khan was pleased to have TRIO agents in the United States. It was the wealthiest, most powerful nation on earth and probably the greatest opponent of international communism. Tosha Khan still hated the Soviet Union. If Moscow feared and despised the United States, then America must not be all bad.

However, Kuming and Tanaka were veterans of the Black Serpent tong and the Snake Clan of the yakuza. Their loyalty was directed toward Wang and Shimo, not Tosha Khan or the New Horde. Despite the merger of the three crime syndicates, everything in TRIO was not equal.

"We have successfully established a new narcotics market in San Francisco," Kuming declared. "TRIO is now in control of approximately eighty-five percent of the heroin trade in the city. O'Malley's syndicate still controls the cocaine and other lesser drugs as well as organized prostitution, illegal gambling and certain other activities."

"But we are working to change that," Tanaka added. "Already we have eliminated most of the Irishman's drug peddlers on the street."

"We know of this from a radio report," Shimo, the yakuza boss, said grimly. "Blowing up a car in the middle of a busy street is not subtle. It may well attract unwanted attention and cause more trouble than it is worth."

"The police have no reason to suspect us, Shimo-sama," Tanaka assured him, addressing the yakuza chief as "Lord Shimo."

"Indeed," Kuming added. "They know nothing of TRIO."

"That is our greatest strength," Shimo stated. "Our organization is invisible and must remain so. Rash actions endanger our society. We must not move too quickly or we will surely make mistakes, my brothers."

"There is a time for stealth," Tosha Khan agreed. "But there is also a time when bold attack is the only logical strategy. We must strike swiftly at the heart of this Irish don's syndicate. We must strike *now* before he has a chance to retaliate."

"That would be most unwise," Shimo insisted. "Surely you must realize that such an assault on O'Malley's headquarters would cause the police to thoroughly investigate the incident. With enough clues and a bit of luck they could piece together enough information to expose TRIO."

"What Mr. Shimo says has merit," Wang Tse-Tu remarked. "But Mr. Tosha has also raised a valid point. We must consider both sides to make an intelligent decision."

"Yin and yang?" Tosha Khan asked, barely concealing his contempt for Chinese philosophy. The Mongols had conquered the Chinese because Genghis Khan had been a general, not a philosopher.

"Everything has an opposite," Wang said calmly. He often considered it a waste of time to explain anything to Tosha. Mongolians were always barbarians and they always would be. "We must maintain balance. That is the natural order of things. When man ignores this balance and fails to consider the yin as well as the yang, then he opens the pit to his own downfall."

"Please, Mr. Wang," the Khan sighed. "This is not the time to discuss—"

"Please let me finish," the tong leader urged. "I was about to say that we should consider advantages and disadvantages, the value of our goal and the risk of the enterprise. Personally I feel our best defense against O'Malley is a most aggressive offense."

"Then you believe we should order a full-scale attack on O'Malley's headquarters, Mr. Wang?" Shimo asked with a frown.

"We have two immediate concerns, my brothers," Wang replied. "The Irishman's syndicate on one hand and the police on the other. O'Malley is clearly the more immediate threat. The police will have to collect considerable evidence before they'll make a move against us. The Irishman will not need justification, search warrants or legal permission to act against us."

"Mr. Wang," Shimo said. "Gang warfare is very dangerous because it will incite the anger of the public. This was demonstrated in this very country in the past. May I remind you of the gang wars between Capone and Moran in the 1930s?"

"Tactfully you did not mention the tong wars that occurred in New York at the turn of the century," Wang said with a small smile. "Or those that occurred in this very city in the 1850s, although I'm certain you thought of them, as well."

"Lessons can be learned by recalling the mistakes of others," the yakuza boss suggested.

"That is an intelligent observation, Mr. Shimo," the Chinese master criminal said with a nod. "But I still feel we should strike while O'Malley is off guard."

"Gentlemen," Tosha Khan began, "may I remind you that the man known as the Executioner smashed the Mafia and fragmented the powers of organized crime in this country? Yet according to our intelligence reports the Colombian syndicate and some Mexican hoodlums have joined the Irishman's mob. The Mafia might be getting results from such Latin gangs to build up its manpower. We must strike before they can recover from the beating the Executioner gave them."

"True," Wang agreed. "We have no choice. We must destroy O'Malley's headquarters and quickly. Kuming? Tanaka? Do you both understand what must be done now?"

"We understand," Harold Kuming replied.

"We shall see to the destruction of the Irishman's headquarters," Andrew Tanaka added. "And we'll make certain O'Malley is dead."

"Han hau," Wang replied. "Very good. We shall leave the matter in your most capable hands."

"My associates and I have business elsewhere," Shimo stated. The yakuza leader had reluctantly accepted the decision of his fellow TRIO commanders. "But I believe you have more than two hundred TRIO enforcers in the San Francisco area. Use as many men as necessary to accomplish your mission."

"Hai, Shimo-sama," Tanaka said with a bow. "It shall be done."

7

Calvin James and Rafael Encizo met the other members of Phoenix Force in a Holiday Inn hotel room. They had assembled in this unlikely meeting place to avoid sharing information with Alex Trumball and the Department of Justice. James and Encizo told their partners about the information they acquired from Leon.

"Your informer's story agrees with what Agent Trumball told us," Gary Manning said, pouring himself a cup of black coffee. "This O'Malley appears to be an adopted child of the Mafia. Apparently he's risen quite high in the ranks of the Family."

"Not the Mafia," Katz corrected as he tapped the steel hooks of his prosthesis on the glass top of the coffee table. "This is a MERGE operation."

"Sure looks that way," James agreed. "With the Colombian syndicate and the Mexican Mafia involved, as well."

"Yeah," Encizo added, working the blade of his *tanto* knife along a whetstone with a thin coat of oil. "But I sort of wonder about the Orientals Leon mentioned. Seems strange for the mob to hire Chinese henchmen."

"MERGE operates a bit differently than the Mafia," David McCarter commented, lighting a Players cigarette. "La Cosa Nostra wouldn't have formed a partnership with the Hispanic syndicates, either. Maybe MERGE has an equal-opportunity program."

"Well," Manning said with a shrug, "I think we

know where the head of the octopus is this time. Why don't we make straight for it and save time?''

"O'Malley appears to be the top dog in San Francisco crime," Katz agreed. "What puzzles me is why did the heroin delivery come directly from the Orient? MERGE has contacts within the Corsican syndicate. They refine heroin in France and ship it here, either directly or through sources south of the border.''

"Maybe we'll find some answers after we take care of O'Malley," McCarter suggested. "The bloke is obviously with MERGE. Putting his operation out of order falls under the category of things to do on our mission.''

"The cops haven't been able to get enough evidence on O'Malley to lock his ass in jail," James remarked. "And frankly, I don't think we have enough proof to justify launching a full-scale assault on the Irish don, either.''

"So let's get some evidence," Encizo suggested. "Didn't Trumball give you guys the blueprints to O'Malley's house?''

"We've got blueprints for where he lives," McCarter answered. "But it isn't exactly a house. It's an office building, ten stories high and half a block in diameter. This doesn't include the parking lot and lawn surrounding the place.''

"He lives there?" James asked with surprise.

"He owns the building and manages to write the whole place off as a tax deduction," Katz answered. "Of course, it houses a number of legitimate businesses, most of which belong to O'Malley. Legal firms, real estate offices, stockbrokers are all located there. He even has a spa and a dentist.''

"And he also has a private security force exclusively for the building," McCarter added. "Chaps work there twenty-four hours a day. Naturally they're licensed to carry firearms. Corridors inside are monitored by closed-circuit television cameras.''

"I imagine O'Malley does most of his business there," Encizo mused.

"Almost exclusively," Katz confirmed. "In fact, O'Malley rarely leaves the building for any reason. Of course he has virtually everything he needs in there."

"Sounds like we should carry out a soft probe on the place," Encizo continued. "But soft probes can turn hard fast. What about innocent bystanders?"

"O'Malley is divorced," Katz replied. "According to all information Trumball has on the office building, all the real-estate agents, dentists, secretaries and cleaning personnel are out of the place by 8:00 P.M. Only one lawyer usually stays after closing hours. His name is Arthur Fucci, and he's O'Malley's personal attorney."

"You mean his *consigliere*?" James muttered.

"That's what the cops and the Justice boys figure," Manning confirmed. "Fucci handles most of O'Malley's business deals that are legit and probably most of the stuff that isn't."

"A low-life in a three-piece suit is still a low-life," James growled. "They're even worse than the dudes without the fancy education because they can't even plead ignorance."

"Penetrating security at O'Malley's building isn't going to be easy," Manning said. "Besides the cameras, they've got guards patrolling the corridors inside and sentries on foot patrolling outside, as well. Now these guys are not your typical rent-a-cops. No old retired postmen or college kids who are trying to subsidize a chickenshit income. These fellas get paid fifteen dollars an hour, and they don't get that kind of money for goofing off. They're all young enough to have good reflexes and experienced enough to be professionals. As far as we can find out, they're all military veterans, most with a less-than-honorable discharge. Every four months they have to go to the firing range to hone their marksmanship. They're also trained in stick defense and some fundamental hand-to-hand combat. Guards are armed with .357 Magnums, nightsticks and mace."

"Of course," Katz said. "We all have experience at taking out sentries, but we don't want to kill anyone on a soft probe unless it's absolutely necessary. Taking out a large number of well-armed, well-trained men without using lethal force isn't going to be easy."

"As if that isn't bad enough," Manning added, "the windows and outside doors are wired to a burglar-alarm system. Point of interest: it only alerts the personnel inside the building. No link to the police department. I guess O'Malley likes to handle intruders without interference from the authorities."

"That's actually in our favor," Encizo remarked. "We don't want to have to worry about the cops getting involved, either. Every security system has a weakness. Any idea what O'Malley's might be?"

"Yeah," Manning replied. "The roof. Not much of a weakness, mind you, but there aren't any sentries posted there. Now when we get inside, the air-conditioning system has large vents and ducts and the shafts are big enough for a man to crawl through. We can tunnel all through the place, providing we're all willing to make like Santa Claus for a while."

"Sounds like we've just about got this thing licked," James commented cheerfully.

"Don't celebrate too soon," the Canadian warned. "The main guard station is on the bottom floor, but the apartments on the tenth floor include a number of guards' quarters as well as rooms for some of O'Malley's gangster cronies. O'Malley and some of his personal bodyguards live on the eighth floor. But the worst problem about the roof is it's cluttered with pigeon coops. Believe it or not, O'Malley has some guy who trains carrier pigeons.''

''There's no way I can land a helicopter on the roof, anyway,'' McCarter, the ace pilot, remarked. ''Too many blokes outside to see it coming. Besides, those rotor blades aren't quiet. Chaps on the tenth floor would hear us for sure.''

''And even you couldn't land a glider on a surface that narrow and that crowded,'' Manning told the Briton. ''But don't take that as a challenge. You damn near got us killed when you landed that glider on a goddamn helicopter pad last month.''

''We can't parachute in,'' James added. ''We'd be more apt to get splattered all over a wall or blown off course to the bay.''

''Maybe we can float to the roof,'' McCarter suggested.

''We'd have to use a lot of bubble gum,'' James responded with a snort. ''Or do we tie a bunch of helium balloons to our belts?''

''As a matter of fact,'' the Briton said, smiling, ''that's pretty close to what I have in mind. Did you chaps know that the first successful aircraft were hot-air balloons?''

''Jesus,'' Manning groaned. ''You can't be serious, David. Those balloons are enormous. One of those big bastards would attract more attention than a Sherman tank.''

''A *big* balloon with a large basket attached would,'' McCarter agreed. ''But a couple of smaller balloons wouldn't be nearly as obvious, especially if the bags were black and the men attached to them wore black, too.''

"This sounds like another one of your crazy ideas, David," James muttered.

"Some of his crazy ideas have worked in the past," Katz reminded the others. "Let's hear it, David."

THE GELLER TRADE BUILDING was located on Market Street, two and a half blocks from O'Malley Enterprises. As Katz, McCarter and Encizo stood on the roof, the Israeli took a small digital watch from his pocket. It was a quarter past midnight.

"Zero fifteen on the nose," Katz announced.

McCarter and Encizo synchronized watches.

All three men were dressed in black, but Katz wore a dark blue Windbreaker, as well. It concealed a Sig-Sauer P-226 pistol in shoulder leather. Encizo carried an H&K MP-5 machine pistol and an S&W M-59 autoloader. McCarter had his favorite weapons, an M-10 Ingram and a Browning Hi-Power. All five firearms were 9mm parabellum caliber. The Cuban and the Briton also carried Bio-Inoculator pistols.

McCarter and Encizo wore rather bulky backpacks with sturdy harnesses, similar to parachute rigs, buckled around their torsos. The packs contained four-gallon butane tanks. The nozzles were attached to black rubber bags covered with thick nylon netting. Copper tubing extended from the tanks to valves hooked to their belts. Both men also carried radio transceivers and an assortment of grenades and ammo pouches.

Encizo's *tanto* was strapped to his left ankle and a number of *shaken* throwing stars were in a pouch on his belt. The Cuban was an expert with a knife and his skill had been further developed as a student of *tanto-jutsu*.

The late Keio Ohara, one of the original five men of Phoenix Force, had first instructed Encizo in this little-known martial art. The *tanto* had been the fighting knife of the samurai, and the Cuban's Cold Steel blade was a modern version of this honored weapon.

Ohara had also introduced Encizo to the Japanese art of *shuriken-jutsu*. The true *shuriken* is a throwing spike, difficult to master, requiring many hours of practice to perfect. The star-shaped *shaken* is easier to manipulate and generally more accurate. With four or more sharp points, the *shaken* will almost certainly stick in a target every time. Encizo proved to be a superb student and soon surpassed his teacher's skill in both *tanto-jutsu* and *shuriken-jutsu*.

"All right," Katzenelenbogen said. "One more time. David, are you absolutely certain these balloon contraptions will work?"

"I'm positive, Yakov," McCarter replied confidently. "These compact aerostats are safe as houses. I've never used this sort of rig before, but I've operated a couple larger hot-air balloons in the past, and they all work on the same principles. I'm sure I can handle it."

"I wish I felt the same way," Encizo muttered.

"If you don't want to do this, Rafael," Katz said, "you don't have to. It isn't too late to cancel the probe. Frankly, I think we've been rushing into this too quickly. I'd rather we spent some more time putting together a plan."

"I'd have to be loco if I *wanted* to do this," Encizo said. "But I think we should go ahead with the probe. We need some answers, and we know where to get them. I just happen to be the logical choice to sail into the vile blue yonder with David. I can take out the alarms, pick locks and so forth, and I've also done some hang gliding in the past. David tells me this is sort of similar."

"Actually ballooning is safer than hang gliding," McCarter assured him.

"I hope so," the Cuban admitted. "To be honest, hang gliding scared the hell out of me."

"Then I guess it's settled," Katz said, still a bit reluctant. "Remember to maintain radio contact. We won't transmit unless we receive a message from you first. Tinny little voices coming from a radio could seriously reduce your ability to sneak up behind a sentry. Of course, this is a soft probe. We don't want any killing unless there's no way to avoid it."

"It'd be nice if we could count on O'Malley's blokes to share that sentiment," McCarter commented.

"If the soft probe goes hard, the rest of us will be ready to charge in to assist," the Israeli promised. "Give me enough time to join the others before you lift off. Zero one hundred hours will be ideal. Give us a call when you're ready to move."

"Affirmative," McCarter replied.

"Take care," the Phoenix Force commander told them, genuinely concerned about two men whom he loved as brothers. "And good luck."

8

It was 0100 hours.

"Okay, mates," McCarter said into his transceiver. "You read me? Over."

"Loud and clear," Gary Manning replied from the radio. "Over."

"We're about to become fly-by-nights," the Briton announced. "Over."

"Go for it," Manning's voice answered. "Over and out."

Two dark figures rose into the night sky. McCarter and Encizo dangled from nylon cords suspended from the great black spheres of two inflated balloons, each about twelve feet in diameter. The Phoenix Force pair gradually floated higher as they turned up the butane to feed more fuel to the burner attached to the hoop at the mouth of the bag.

Rafael Encizo understood the basic principles of hot-air balloons. An aerostat is a vessel that uses the buoyancy in air the way a ship uses water. The Montgolfier brothers flew the first hot-air balloon in 1783. According to legend, Joseph Montgolfier had noticed smoke rise from the fire that destroyed his father's paper mill. He reasoned if hot air rises through cool air, then hot air in a bag would also rise.

And so the hot-air balloon was developed. Simple, logical and relatively uncomplicated compared to a plane or a helicopter. But as he floated away from the

Geller Building, Rafael Encizo wished the hot-air balloon had never been invented. The Cuban did not like trusting his life to a rubber bag full of heated air.

McCarter did not seem worried, but everybody knew McCarter was crazy. He actually *liked* being shot at. The Briton enjoyed risking his life, but he never put his teammates in unnecessary danger. If McCarter said the balloons were safe, then they were safe.

The current of the wind remained favorable as they drifted toward O'Malley Enterprises. McCarter had assured Encizo that they could steer the balloons by opening vents in the bags. Gas would eject from portholes to alter the direction of flight. A sudden hard wind could blow them too far off course and then they would be forced to land elsewhere.

Encizo glanced down at the street below. The sensation was similar to a ski lift or sky tram. Cars and pedestrians seemed smaller, but the view was not terribly dramatic from less than two hundred feet.

The sensation of drifting was rather pleasant, almost dreamlike. The roar of the burner was comforting after Encizo quit worrying about the balloon catching fire. The heat from the mouth of the bag felt like an oven overhead, but Encizo found the balloon flight to be less frightening than hang gliding or skydiving. It was like traveling by parachute with more control of movement.

The Cuban was so fascinated by the trip that he did not realize they were directly over O'Malley Enterprises until he noticed McCarter had begun to descend. Encizo worked the valves slowly, gradually leaking gas from the bag and reducing the fuel to the burner. Gravity did the rest. The Cuban floated to the roof and landed gently on his feet near a column of pigeon coops.

"Cut the fuel off," McCarter said sharply. "The burner will set the bag on fire if you don't."

Encizo obeyed immediately, and the balloon deflated quickly. McCarter stripped off his harness and helped his partner with the straps to his rig. Encizo grinned at the Briton.

"This was one of your better ideas, David," he said.

"Glad you approve," McCarter replied. "Now that we're here, it's time for you to do your break-and-enter tricks, amigo. I hope you remembered your burglar tools."

"I've got my kit right here," the Cuban assured him, patting his jacket. "Don't leave home without it."

They moved to the door casing of a garret. Encizo knelt by the door and took a compact leather packet from inside his jacket. He opened the case to reveal an assortment of lock picks and metal probes, and he selected a thin probe and an instrument that resembled a surgeon's scalpel. Encizo carefully inserted the probe at the door near the bottom hinge.

"I hope the information on the wiring of this place is accurate," he whispered. "The primary burglar-alarm system is supposed to be pretty simple. The door is wired to set off a signal when it's opened. Pressure activated. Cut the wires and kill the alarm. Primitive system considering the state of the art nowadays."

"The wiring is at the hinge?" McCarter inquired.

"That's how it's usually done," Encizo replied, working the probe along the crack. "Some burglars will try to remove the pins from the hinges to get through a door. Even if the hinges are on the inside, it isn't too hard to do if you have the right tools."

"You obviously had a misspent youth, Rafael." The Briton chuckled. "I always knew we had something in common."

"Okay," Encizo announced. "I got it."

He slipped in the thin blade of the scalpel and carefully cut the wires. Encizo returned the tools to his kit and selected two lock picks. He inserted them into the keyhole and gingerly worked the picks until the lock clicked. He turned the knob and opened the door.

The Cuban drew his Bio-Inoculator pistol. A powerful air gun, the B-I pistol was a one-shot weapon loaded with a tranquilizer dart. Encizo held the sleep gun close to his side, next to the Heckler & Koch blaster that hung from his shoulder. Some situations demand full-auto death, and Encizo wanted to be ready to grab his machine pistol PDQ if needed. McCarter followed his example and held his Bio-Inoculator close to the Ingram M-10.

"Nighthawk One," Encizo spoke into the transceiver. "This is Nighthawk Two. Over."

"Nighthawk Two," Gary Manning's voice replied from the radio. "Glad somebody remembered the code names. Over."

"We're going inside," the Cuban announced. "Keep your ears up. Over."

"Affirmative," Manning stated. "Watch your ass. Over."

"Makes my neck stiff," Encizo said. "But we'll try. Over and out."

They entered the garret and descended a narrow stairwell to the story below. When the Cuban reached the door at the bottom, he flicked on a penlight and checked for alarm wires. He found none. Encizo took out his set of lock picks and went to work on the door.

Within seconds, he had picked the lock, and he turned the knob and slowly pushed it open just enough to peer out with one eye. He saw a uniformed figure less than a yard away. The guard stared at the door, uncertain whether it had actually moved or not. His hand hovered by the Magnum revolver on his hip.

Encizo did not hesitate. He immediately threw the door open and attacked. The Cuban's boot lashed out, kicking the startled guard between the legs before he could draw his side arm. The man uttered an ugly choking cough as he doubled up. Encizo's left hand snaked out and seized the guard's hair to pull him forward.

The Cuban's right hand grabbed the doorknob while he hauled the guy's head to the doorframe. Then he yanked the door hard and slammed it against the guard's skull. The man's knees buckled and he began to sag. Encizo quickly pulled him across the threshold. He chopped the edge of his hand into the side of the guard's neck to be certain he was unconscious.

"I hate it when things like this happen," the Cuban muttered as he shut the door.

"I bet he didn't care for it, either," McCarter commented, helping Encizo with the senseless guard.

They bound the sentry's wrists and ankles with plastic riot cuffs and gagged the poor bastard. Encizo checked the corridor again. He saw blue walls and green carpet but no sign of other sentries.

His attention was drawn to a metal-and-plastic object jutting from a stalk on the wall. As the camera slowly scanned the hallway, Encizo eased the door shut and turned to McCarter.

"City camera out there," he told the Briton. "Pretty small target. You'd better handle it."

"Where is it?" McCarter inquired, drawing his Browning pistol and taking a nine-inch sound suppressor from a pocket.

Encizo gave him the details as the Briton fitted the silencer to the threaded muzzle of his Hi-Power. McCarter eased the door open and watched the camera slowly rotate. When the lens was facing the other way, McCarter raised his Browning and aimed.

The camera was less than a foot long and ten feet from the door. A damn tough target for a handgun equipped with a silencer, but David McCarter had once been on the British Olympic pistol team. He had not participated in the games because his duty to the SAS transferred him to Oman at the time. McCarter altered the aim slightly to compensate for the silencer.

He triggered the Browning twice. Both 9mm parabellum rounds smashed into the camera. Metal and plastic exploded and the lens popped off and fell to the floor. Scratch one camera, the Briton thought as he opened the door, and he and Encizo stepped through. The hall was still deserted.

"Whoever's watching the monitors is bound to notice this camera isn't transmitting anymore," McCarter commented. "They'll probably send somebody to find out why not."

"Providing they didn't already see me take out the sentry," Encizo added. "In which case there'll be a dozen guards hunting us. I'm afraid Katz was right. We rushed into this, David. We should have spent more time planning the assault."

"Well, we're here now," McCarter said with a shrug. "Let's play out the hand we dealt ourselves and wrap up this recon as quick as we can."

"Let me check the map," Encizo said, unfolding a chart of the building. "An air-conditioning vent large enough for us to enter should be located near the elevators."

"Where the hell are the elevators?" the Briton wondered aloud.

"This way," Encizo replied, tilting his head to the right. "I think."

They moved through the corridor. To their great relief and moderate surprise, the Phoenix pair found the elevators. The air-conditioning vent was located around the corner. Encizo removed a screwdriver from his belt and prepared to take the bolts from the wire-mesh cover of the vent.

"Heads up," McCarter rasped when he heard the rumble of gears inside an elevator shaft. "Company coming up."

"Yeah," the Cuban agreed. "Let's say hello."

The doors of an elevator rolled open with an electrical hum. Two men stepped from the car. One held a canvas tool bag in one fist while his other hand rested on the grips of his holstered revolver. The other man held a Marlin lever-action rifle.

McCarter and Encizo were waiting for them on each side of the doors. The guards started to cross the threshold and the Phoenix commandos pounced. McCarter's left hand shoved the barrel of the Marlin toward the floor as he jammed the muzzle of his silenced Browning under the gunman's chin.

"Drop it or you're dead," the Briton snarled.

The man let the Marlin fall to the floor. Encizo had seized the other guard from behind, grabbing the man's throat with one hand while he stuck the muzzle of his Bio-Inoculator against the base of the guy's skull.

"Hand away from the gun," the Cuban instructed. "Don't raise it. Hold your arm out to the side. Drop the bag and raise the other arm the same way. Don't get cute. We know any tricks you might be familiar with, so don't try anything."

Neither guard resisted. McCarter and Encizo ordered the flunkies to face a wall and spread-eagle, and they stripped the guards of their weapons. Both men carried walkie-talkies.

"The guy we jumped in the hall wasn't carrying one of these," Encizo remarked. "You fellas must have been sent to see what happened to the camera and then call down with the information, right?''

"Yeah," the man who had carried the bag answered. "And I'd repair it if it was just a minor malfunction."

"Okay," the Cuban said, handing him a radio. "Call your control and tell him you found the camera. It's shorted out. A couple of wires are fused together. It'll take a while to repair, but nothing to worry about. You got that?''

"I got it," the guard assured him.

"And no cute little key phrases to let them know you're in trouble, either," McCarter warned. "If anything sounds even a bit odd, you and your mate are dead men.''

"Take a deep breath and settle your nerves," Encizo advised. "Then make the call."

The guard obeyed instructions to the letter. McCarter swapped his Browning for the Bio-Inoculator and aimed his sleep gun at one guard while Encizo covered the other with his own B-I pistol.

"You fellas get to live," Encizo remarked as he squeezed the trigger of his nonlethal weapon.

The air gun hissed like a serpent, and one of the guards yelped from the sting of a steel dart in his left thigh. The other man uttered a similar cry of alarm when McCarter pumped a dart into his leg.

"Don't worry," Encizo assured them. "It's just a tranquilizer. Get your butts down the corridor before you pass out.''

Both guards had received 150 milligrams of thorazine, and they began to stagger when they were only halfway down the hall. McCarter and Encizo had to drag the half-conscious pair to the door in order to hide them with the first sentry. They cuffed and gagged the sleeping guards before returning to the air-conditioning vent.

Encizo soon opened the screen, and they crawled through the four-by-four gap. With the aid of penlights and the map of the building, the pair slowly crawled through yards and yards of aluminum duct work until they reached a junction that branched down to the next story. McCarter and Encizo worked their way down the shaft, bracing their feet against one side and their backs against the other.

The mountaineering "chimney-climb" technique allowed them to descend to the next level. Voices echoed from the tubing, and they froze, listening for identifiable sounds beyond the rapid thunder of their own hearts.

They crawled toward the sound. A patch of light helped guide them to the source of the voices. Encizo advanced first, slithering on his belly as he approached a vent and peered through the screen.

Four men were seated at a long walnut table. A crystal decanter of wine sat in the center of the table, and three of the men smoked large cigars. Havana cigars, Encizo realized, recognizing the aroma of the smoke. The man at the head of the table was heavily built with carrot-colored hair and wide features. Encizo was certain he was looking at Ian O'Malley—the Irish don.

"We've been discussing this business for half an hour and you still haven't told us what you intend to do," a swarthy man with a pitted face told O'Malley. "My best man, Montoya, was killed. Blown to bits by these damn slant-eyed devils. And you do nothing!"

"Me?" O'Malley glared at him. "What are you layin' all this shit on me for, Gomez? MERGE is suppose to be a cooperative business. Right? You fuckin' Colombians had better start carryin' your own weight instead of expectin' the Mafia to carry you."

"MERGE would not have a cocaine trade if it wasn't for the Colombian syndicate," Gomez declared. "Don't try to dodge your responsibilities, O'Malley. This is your city. You are the man in charge of operations here. No?"

"None of us can dodge our responsibilities," a beefy man with olive skin and a wrinkled beetle brow commented. "And we all have suffered because of these Chinese killers."

Juan Alverez, Encizo thought, recognizing the fat man. Alverez was a kingpin in the Mexican mafia. He had formerly been the top dog in the illegal gambling rackets in Texas. Dogfights, cockfights and matches between boys and men without rules. Alverez had made a fortune by appealing to the blood lust of others before he had been forced to flee Texas. Encizo had occasionally wondered where the Mexican hoodlum had found sanctuary. Now he knew.

"The gooks never pulled anythin' like this before," O'Malley stated. "Supposedly the chinks have a syndicate of some sort, but they've never fucked with the mob before."

"They probably assume the Mafia is washed up," Gomez snickered. "And maybe they're right."

"Listen, you spic smartass," O'Malley began tensely. "If all you can do is run your mouth, we don't need you."

"I haven't seen you do anything but talk," Gomez said with a smile.

"Calm down, gentlemen," the fourth man urged. He was small, with a dark brown goatee and wire-rimmed glasses. The fellow looked more like a European psychologist than a gangster. "Let's not fight with one another. These Orientals are the enemy. *Oui?*"

"The chinks wouldn't be musclin' us if they hadn't gained strength and connections by havin' a monopoly on the heroin market," O'Malley complained. "You Corsican syndicate boys were supposed to get a big shipment to us. It never arrived, De Gault."

"That wasn't the fault of the Union de Corse," De Gault said stiffly. "Our entire MERGE network in the Bahamas was ruined. We can only guess what went wrong there. Perhaps they also bickered too much with one another."

Encizo was astonished to discover a MERGE conference in progress. Phoenix Force could not have expected to be so lucky. He was equally surprised by how poorly O'Malley was handling command. The Irishman might be a good businessman, but he certainly was an incompetent general.

But who the hell had declared war on MERGE? The Oriental gangsters were clearly rivals. That meant someone other than MERGE was responsible for the new supply of heroin in San Francisco and the slaughter of the Coast Guard personnel. But who were they?

Suddenly a siren wailed. The intensity of the sound vibrated through the air-conditioning system, suggesting the alarm was bellowing all over the building. O'Malley jumped from his chair and yanked a snubnosed revolver from a belt holster. The Colombian and Mexican gangsters followed his example and also unsheathed pistols. De Gault sat paralyzed, frightened and confused.

"Good Lord," the Corsican whined. "What's going on?"

"Get off your ass, you frog shithead," O'Malley growled. "Somebody's broken into the building, damn it!"

Encizo glanced over his shoulder at McCarter. The

Briton's expression revealed he was aware what the alarm meant.

"I take it the shit has hit the proverbial fan," Mc-Carter whispered.

"By the bucketful," Encizo confirmed.

9

Rafael Encizo and David McCarter naturally assumed the alarm had been triggered because the security personnel had discovered they had broken into the building.

They were wrong.

A furniture van had smashed through the gate to the parking lot of O'Malley Enterprises. The guards patrolling outside the building had already been dispatched, silently killed by knife or garrote. The van continued across the lot to the side entrance of the building where two men jumped out of the vehicle and rushed to the door. Using a low-velocity plastic explosion to blast the door open with a minimum of noise, the pair waved to the van. Two dozen armed men emerged from the back of the vehicle and charged to the entrance.

"Jesus!" Calvin James exclaimed as he watched the black-clad invaders swarm into the building. "What the hell is going on?"

James, Katz and Manning were stationed in a television-repair truck across the street from O'Malley Enterprises. The interior contained an assortment of sophisticated surveillance equipment, including a long-range microphone with a sound-amplification receiver and a transceiver radio that allowed them to stay in contact with McCarter and Encizo. James was peering through an infrared periscope when he saw the assault force from the van storm O'Malley's headquarters.

"Looks like somebody else is interested in the Irish don," Gary Manning remarked, gazing through another night viewer. "And they're even less patient than we are."

"What do the invaders look like?" Katz demanded as he reached for his Uzi submachine gun.

"Can't tell," the Canadian replied, still gazing into a periscope. "They're dressed in black outfits, similar to those ninja uniforms the Tigers of Justice wore. Some of them are carrying Oriental weapons, too. Swords, *nunchaku, sai...*"

"Are they Orientals?" the Israeli asked sharply.

"Wait a second," James said as he adjusted his scope to get a better view of the two men seated in the cab of the van. The driver was a thin Chinese with slicked-down hair. The guy next to him looked like a sumo wrestler in street clothes. "Affirmative, Yakov."

"What's the..." Manning began. Suddenly he knew what Katz was thinking. "My God, we've been chasing the wrong bunch of crooks."

"David and Rafael are in there," the Israeli declared. "They're right in the middle of that mess. Come on, gentlemen, let's go crash the party."

"Hope they've got enough onion dip to go around," James commented as he scrambled to the driver's seat and slid behind the wheel.

Within seconds, the TV-repair truck pulled away from the curb, swung a fast U-turn and sped into the parking lot of O'Malley Enterprises. Several black-clad assassins, the men who had silently killed the guard patrol, were still lurking in the lot. They did not know who was in the truck that had just charged onto the scene, but they did not think real TV repairmen made house calls at two o'clock in the morning.

One of the hit men raised a .380 Sterling automatic

with a silencer attached to the muzzle and opened fire on the windshield. The 95-grain projectile lost considerable velocity when it passed through the sound suppressor, and when the slug struck the curved glass surface it bounced off without even cracking the windshield.

James ignored the ping of the impact and steered the truck toward the furniture van. Another assassin aimed an M-11 Ingram at the rear tires and squeezed the trigger. A burst of .380 rounds spat from the weapon's silencer. The gunman wasn't familiar with the different pattern of bullets caused by the sound suppressor. Bullets sparked against concrete and ricocheted along the steel skin of the truck without causing any real damage.

The gunmen chased after the speeding truck, holding their fire, waiting for a clear target. Col. Yakov Katzenelenbogen saw the pair of gun-toting shadows jog up behind the vehicle. The Israeli unlatched the rear door and braced his Uzi across his prosthetic arm.

A solid kick threw the door open, and the gunmen stared into the silencer-equipped muzzle of the Israeli's submachine gun. Katz opened fire, hosing the pair with 9mm projectiles. The killers jerked and contorted in wild spasms of death, and then collapsed to the pavement, their torsos oozing blood.

The truck came to a screeching halt when James stomped on the brake as the vehicle drew closer to the enemy van. The Chinese driver leaped from his vehicle and aimed a pistol at the truck. James swung open the door and slithered out. The enemy pistolman triggered his weapon, a .357 AutoMag with a stainless-steel silencer, and the powerful 158-grain projectile pierced the windshield and punched into the upholstery of the backrest behind the steering wheel, where Calvin James had been just two seconds before.

The black commando leaned under the open door of the truck and aimed his Colt Commander at the Chinese gunman. The enemy had turned his attention toward the open door and altered the aim of his AutoMag accordingly. James fired his Colt before the Chinese killer could trigger his weapon.

The big Commander roared. James had not had time to fit a silencer to the pistol, and flames spewed from the muzzle like the breath of a miniature dragon. A .45-caliber hollowpoint slug punctured the Chinese button-man's stomach.

The enemy gunman doubled up and fell to his knees, but he still held the big steel AutoMag in his fist. James fired the .45 auto again. The second 185-grain HP round nailed the Chinese killer in the center of the chest. The slug burst his sternum into shrapnel that ripped into heart and lungs. The assassin pitched forward on his face, dead.

Katz jumped out of the rear of the truck, Uzi held ready. He glimpsed another dark figure moving among the shadows and the Israeli swung his subgun at the ominous shape. His black-clad opponent swung an arm, and Katz instinctively ducked. A throwing star sailed over the Israeli's head and clanged against the metal skin of the truck.

The Phoenix Force commander blasted a 3-round volley into the aggressor, and a scream of agony rewarded his effort as the killer tumbled to the ground, a *shaken* star clenched in his fist.

Another enemy in black emerged from the shadows and aimed a pistol at Katz's back. Gary Manning had stepped from the passenger side of the truck, a Heckler & Koch MP-5 machine pistol in his fists. The Canadian opened fire on the assassin and parabellum bullets coughed from the sound suppressor attached to his weapon. The volley slammed into the killer's torso, lifting the man off his feet and hurling him back into the shadows to die.

Manning saw a sudden movement from the corner of his eye. He whirled, but the killer had already slipped behind him, and a wire loop swung over the Canadian's head. He quickly jammed the muzzle of his H&K next to his own neck as the garrote tightened.

The assassin yanked the wooden handles of his weapon hard, but the gun barrel blocked the wire and prevented the man from throttling Manning. The Canadian held the machine pistol, pressing against the wire as he rammed an elbow into his opponent's ribs. Manning was built like a bull moose and he hit like a jackhammer. The killer gasped painfully as a rib cracked. Manning stomped a boot heel on the assailant's instep and drove another elbow stroke to the goon's rib cage.

The killer's grip on the garrote weakened, and Manning thrust the H&K forward, ripping the garrote from his opponent's grasp. The Canadian suddenly ducked and rammed his elbow into the assassin's groin. The man convulsed in agony as Manning slid an arm between the aggressor's legs and suddenly slung him over his shoulders in an airplane spin.

Manning pivoted and dashed the attacker to the ground. The man landed with a spine-jarring crash, his breath spewing from tortured lungs. Then the Canadian raised a boot and stomped the edge of his foot into the assassin's throat, crushing his windpipe. Blood gushed from the man's gaping mouth, splashing crimson across the toe of Manning's boot.

Calvin James had hastily returned his Colt Commander to its holster and grabbed a Smith & Wesson Model 76 submachine gun from the cab of the truck. As he charged toward the entrance of O'Malley Enterprises, a black figure appeared at the door and aimed a Mini-14 autorifle at James. The black commando triggered his M-76 and the silencer attached to his S&W chatterbox hissed as he stitched a column of 9mm bullet holes up the gunman's torso from navel to throat. The killer dropped his Mini-14 and tumbled across the threshold.

Suddenly a large figure rushed forward from the side of the furniture van. James started to turn, but powerful hands grabbed his M-76 and pulled him off balance. The black warrior landed on his back hard as his opponent wrenched the S&W blaster from his hands. James recognized his assailant. It was the big guy who had been seated next to the driver of the van. The bastard had slipped out the passenger side and waited for a chance to jump one of the Phoenix Force team. Calvin James was the closest target so he was elected for ambush.

The burly Japanese did not waste time fumbling for the trigger. He swung the M-76 like a club, trying to crack James's skull with the wire stock. The black man shifted his head to avoid the attack, and the metal buttstock stamped the pavement next to James's ear. He immediately braced himself on his left hand and slashed the back of his right fist across the muscle man's jaw. The Japanese hardly grunted from the blow.

James swung a tae kwon-do foot-sword kick to the Oriental's ribs, and the big Japanese fell to one knee, growling more in anger than pain. James shifted his position and lashed a circular kick, slamming the back of his heel to the aggressor's skull. The Oriental hulk groaned as the S&W subgun slipped from his grasp.

Calvin James did not intend to give the guy time to recover. He continued to attack, slashing a karate chop at the man's bull neck. But the Japanese came up swinging, and a hard forearm to the chest sent James sprawling. He scrambled to his feet, but the Oriental was already on top of him. The big man bellowed like an enraged ape as he smashed a backhand stroke to James's head. The Phoenix fighter fell against the side of the van, his skull ringing painfully.

Gary Manning rushed to James's aid. The Japanese brute and Calvin were too close together for Manning to open fire with his H&K machine pistol, and the Canadian raised the weapon to butt-stroke the burly thug. The Japanese suddenly whirled and whipped a forearm across Manning's rib cage. The blow jarred the H&K from Manning's hands and knocked him four feet backward.

The Japanese prepared to charge, but Calvin James attacked him from the rear. The black man snapped a stabbing kick to the brute's right kidney and the hulk roared and swung around, sweeping a cross-body karate chop at his tormentor. James ducked under the slashing hand and thrust a palm stroke under the Oriental's jaw.

The big man stumbled backward, right into the arms of Gary Manning. The Canadian wrapped a forearm around the goon's throat and jammed the other arm across the base of his skull. He gripped his own biceps and elbow to form a firm vise around the Japanese thug's neck. Manning slammed a knee to the small of his opponent's back and twisted the man's head with all his might. Vertebrae crunched; Manning had broken the hulk's neck.

"Come on, gentlemen," Katz said sharply as he joined the pair. "Gather up your weapons and let's move."

UNAWARE OF WHAT WAS HAPPENING, Rafael Encizo and David McCarter had already decided on a choice of action against the four MERGE ringleaders in the conference room. The two Phoenix Force commandos had hastily attached silencers to their pistols. Then Encizo crawled into position and kicked the air-conditioning vent as hard as he could.

The screen burst from the wall, and the four startled men in the conference room turned to see McCarter at the vent. Gomez immediately swung his pistol toward the Briton. McCarter's silenced Browning coughed and a 9mm slug smashed into the Colombian's forehead.

Gomez fell lifeless to the floor as O'Malley and Alverez returned fire. Bullets smashed into plaster and punctured aluminum, but McCarter had quickly slithered back from the opening of the vent. Encizo yanked the pin from a flash-bang concussion grenade and lobbed it through the open vent.

The Cuban and Briton covered their ears and screamed to equalize pressure inside their skulls as the grenade exploded. When the sound died away, Encizo thrust his feet through the gap and plunged into the conference room. The concussion blast had tossed furniture in all directions. De Gault, the Corsican, lay on his back. Blood oozed from his ears and mouth. O'Malley was on his knees, both hands clamped over his ears.

Encizo did not see Juan Alverez until the conference table moved. The furniture had been thrown on top of the Mexican gangster, shielding him from the more punishing effects of the explosion. Alverez snarled at Encizo and raised his Star PD .45 auto. The Cuban's S&W autoloader spoke first, rasping two 9mm rounds through the silencer. Alverez caught both bullets squarely in the face. He fell against the table and slumped dead to the floor, the unfired Star still in his fist.

"Adiós, cabrón," Encizo whispered. "The world will be a better place without you."

David McCarter emerged from the vent and slid into the conference room. He took the transceiver from his belt and switched it on while Encizo strolled over to Ian O'Malley and kicked the Irishman's .38 revolver across the floor.

"Nighthawk One, this is Nighthawk Two," McCarter spoke into the radio. "Things are turning hard here. Over."

"No shit, Nighthawk Two," Manning's voice replied. "The place is under attack. Over."

"What the hell?" the Briton muttered. He pressed the transmit button. "Under attack by whom? Over."

"We don't know yet," the Canadian's voice replied. "But they play for keeps. Watch yourselves. These guys aren't on O'Malley's side, but they sure as hell aren't on ours, either. Over."

"Over and out." McCarter switched off the transceiver and turned to Encizo. "Did you hear that?"

"Yeah," the Cuban confirmed. "I think the Irish don's competition has arrived. O'Malley and friends were talking about a gang of Orientals who were screwing up their business."

"And the buggers had to pick tonight to launch an assault on O'Malley's headquarters," McCarter said, rolling his eyes toward the ceiling.

"Why not?" Encizo asked, shrugging. "We did."

The door to the conference room suddenly burst open, and two uniformed guards appeared at the threshold, Magnum revolvers in their fists. They were startled to discover the room was a shambles and they were not expecting to find two armed opponents ready for them. McCarter and Encizo did not hesitate. Their pistols coughed in unison and the two guards fell back into the hallway, bullets drilled through their hearts.

Ian O'Malley was not as dazed as he appeared. The

big Irishman suddenly sprang up from the floor and grabbed for Encizo's pistol. The Cuban's left hand slashed a karate chop under O'Malley's breastbone and snapped a quick backfist to the center of his face. O'Malley staggered back into a wall, blood oozing from his nostrils.

"Just behave," the Cuban warned him.

Another guard appeared at the door, a pump shotgun braced against his hip. McCarter trained his Browning on the man, but a burst of full-auto slugs abruptly smashed into the guard and hurled his bullet-torn corpse into the room.

Two men dressed in black poked the muzzles of machine pistols through the doorway. McCarter and Encizo hesitated, uncertain if the gunmen were other members of Phoenix Force or not. One good look at the hooded figures with almond-shaped eyes above black scarf masks told them the men were not Stony Man personnel.

McCarter and Encizo did not have time to aim and open fire. They instinctively dived to the floor as the gunmen released a tidal wave of full-auto devastation. Bullets sliced through the air and punched into the walls. O'Malley screamed as four slugs ripped into his chest.

As the invaders entered the room, McCarter held his Browning in a two-hand Weaver's grip and squeezed the trigger. A 115-grain missile snapped through the bridge of the first gunman's nose. The bullet knifed through his brain and blasted a gory exit at the back of his skull.

The second gunman swung his Beretta NATO Pistola Mitragliatrice Model 12 toward McCarter. Encizo aimed his S&W and squeezed off two shots. One 9mm round shattered the buttonman's elbow, the other struck his upper arm and tore into the triceps. The M-12 fell from the man's grasp as he shrieked and stumbled into the door frame.

Encizo scrambled to his feet and approached the wounded gunman. The invader pawed at his smashed arm and glared at the Cuban. Without warning, the man shouted a *kiai* war whoop and lashed out a kick. The edge of his foot knocked the M-59 from Encizo's hand.

The killer whirled and launched a high roundhouse kick for the Cuban's head. Encizo dropped to one knee, ducking beneath the flying foot. His hand yanked the Cold Steel *tanto* from its sheath as he rose up behind his opponent, and the Cuban war machine quickly plunged the knife blade into the man's kidney. Encizo's left hand grabbed the invader's shoulder as he pulled the *tanto* from the man's flesh. He quickly drew the razor-sharp edge across the attacker's throat.

"Well," McCarter commented as he gazed at the corpse of Ian O'Malley. "We don't have to worry about the Irish don anymore."

"But we still have to worry about getting out of here alive," Encizo stated, wiping the blood off his knife.

10

Andrew Tanaka and Harold Kuming personally led the TRIO assault on O'Malley Enterprises. The security guards were no match for the professional killer squad armed with full-auto weapons and trained in a variety of Oriental martial arts. Uniformed young men charged into corridors only to be blown into oblivion by merciless volleys of rapid-fire bullets.

The guards were not prepared for gangland combat, but the MERGE buttonmen of Ian O'Malley's personal bodyguard unit were veteran soldiers of the street. Most of these Mafia-bred hardcases had honed their skills with gun, knife and brass knucks during the Bolan wars, just in case they clashed with the Executioner. Some had even studied military tactics and urban warfare.

Two students of advanced mayhem confronted TRIO shock troops on the eighth floor. The pair had invented a simple, but ingenious portable barricade, consisting of a sheet of bulletproof glass bolted to a diner's cart. They rolled the four-by-six shield into the corridor and crouched behind it. Both men were armed with Uzi submachine guns, with plenty of spare ammo.

A half-dozen TRIO invaders prowled the eighth floor, slaughtering security guards and smashing down doors to search rooms for more quarry. The pointman peered around a corner and saw the two MERGE gunmen trying to hide behind a flimsy cart. The TRIO assassins leaped into the corridor and opened fire with machine pistols before they noticed the sheet of shatter-resistant glass.

Bullets slammed into the transparent shield. Cracks formed a road-map pattern in the glass. Several bullets penetrated the barrier. The terms bulletproof and shatter resistant can never be taken too seriously. The MERGE buttonmen stayed low and waited for the TRIO machine gunners to ease their fire.

The invaders stopped shooting and the two MERGE defenders immediately returned fire. Twin columns of 9mm slugs tore into the TRIO hit team. The bullets smashed the life from two Oriental killers and wounded a third before he could dive for cover behind the corner.

"Come on, you fuckers!" one of the MERGE gunsels invited.

"Lots more where that came from!" the other gunman added.

The TRIO troops did not expose themselves to fire. Instead, they lobbed a blue baseball at the MERGE hoods. There were no stitches in the metal sphere because it was actually an M-26 grenade. The miniblaster exploded, tearing the heavy glass sheet to bits. The former shield became a hail of sharp splinters, which sliced into the two MERGE gunmen. Not that this bothered the gunsels. Both men had already been killed by the explosion.

The four survivors of the TRIO hit team exchanged nods of satisfaction with their victory. However, one of the invaders suddenly pointed his Beretta M-12 chopper at a tall lanky black man who had just appeared at the opposite end of the hall.

"Oh, shit," Calvin James muttered when he saw the TRIO assassins swing their weapons in his direction. "Hit it!"

The black commando dropped to the floor after alerting Katz and Manning to danger. The other two Phoenix fighters were around the corner of the corridor and did not see the TRIO assassins. However, James's warning told them to stay down. A salvo of full-auto fire that followed told them why.

Katz and Manning did not intend to leave James pinned down under enemy fire. The Israeli knelt by the corner while Manning stood erect. Both used the edge of the wall for a post bench to steady their weapons as they returned fire at the TRIO gunmen.

Two Oriental killers jumped and convulsed in a wild version of the Last Tango of Death. Their bullet-ravaged bodies tumbled back into the remaining TRIO pair. The survivors jogged behind the cover of the corner closest to their position, startled by the unexpected arrival of the supercommandos of Phoenix Force.

"Thanks, man," James told his partners as he slithered back to their position and rose to his feet. "That was a pretty scary spot, lying on the floor while all those bullets were burning up air above me."

"We know the feeling," Katz assured him. "Rather like having God reminding you of mortality."

"Save the stories," Manning advised, still watching the corridor. "Looks like the bad guys are about to make their move...."

The Canadian's prediction was right on the money. One TRIO gunman poked the barrel of his machine pistol around the corner and fired a hasty volley at the Phoenix Force position. The other Oriental goon pulled the pin from an M-26 and tossed it down the hall. Both TRIO men cowered low and covered their heads, waiting for the grenade to blast their opponents to pieces.

Calvin James suddenly jumped forward and kicked the M-26. It skidded across the floor, bounced against a wall and rolled behind the corner where the TRIO gunsels were lurking. James dived to the floor and covered his head. Katz and Manning followed his example.

Just in time.

The grenade exploded. The TRIO killers were instantly dismembered, beheaded and shredded into bloodied debris. Plaster dust billowed through the corridor as James climbed to his feet, shaking his head to clear it of the dull ringing inside.

"One hell of a field goal, Calvin," Gary Manning told him.

"Yeah," James replied. "I sure wish halftime would come up soon."

"We have to find David and Rafael," Katz declared. "And quickly. The police will be arriving pretty soon and that won't make our job any easier."

"Or any safer," James said.

ANOTHER TEAM OF TRIO INVADERS clashed with a group of MERGE buttonmen on the ninth floor. The battle had erupted inside a small auditorium. The room had been set up for a discussion on the progress of some of Ian O'Malley's businesses, but it had become a slaughter yard. Four MERGE gunmen had retreated into the room as seven TRIO invaders closed in for the kill.

Tables were overturned for cover as the buttonmen fired at the black-clad Orientals. The TRIO troops pinned down their opponents with a lethal stream of full-auto bullets as they charged into the auditorium. Several 9mm slugs punched through flimsy plywood. Two MERGE gunsels screamed when projectiles plowed into their flesh.

Another Mafia vet rose up and fired a sawed-off Stevens side-by-side shotgun. The 12-gauge cannon bellowed. Buckshot crashed into the face and chest of the closest TRIO assassin. The impact of numerous double O buck pellets pulverized the Oriental gunman.

A Japanese killer, born and bred to the yakuza Snake Clan, hurled a *shaken* throwing star. Sharp metal pierced the MERGE shotgunner's chest. He screamed and tried to point his scattergun at his assailant. Another TRIO assassin raised a .38 Colt revolver and triggered two shots.

One 125-grain wadcutter caught the Mafia flunky in the throat. He fell backward, blood spewing from his open mouth. A muscle reaction caused his finger to jerk back the trigger to the second barrel. Buckshot smashed into the mercury light bulbs overhead. A shower of sparks spat from the ceiling as the TRIO killers stalked the fourth and final MERGE defender.

The Mafia enforcer was now alone against six armed opponents, and his only weapon had jammed. The guy figured he would rather die as a ram than a sheep. He grabbed the barrel of his messed-up Thompson subgun and stepped into the open.

"Okay," the hood growled. "I guess you little fuckers got me. Any of you have enough balls to give me a fair fight?"

"Hai," a Japanese thug said, nodding as he reached for the hilt of the sword strapped to his back. "I have balls. Yes?"

"Reckon so," the MERGE hood replied.

He wished he had not made the challenge. The man's sword was almost four feet long and the guy held the weapon as if he knew how to use it. The swordsman approached, the blade of his *katana* poised at eye level. The MERGE hood figured his best chance was to try to bat the sword aside and hope he could slug the Oriental with a back swing.

The buttonman made his move. The stock of the

Thompson whirled at the samurai steel, but the blade moved swiftly. The *katana* ducked under the butt-stroke and the yakuza killer stepped forward. He pivoted smoothly. The motion brought the edge of the sword across his opponent's belly. The MERGE man shrieked as his guts spilled from the long, deep wound.

The Thompson fell from the injured man's grasp. The Japanese raised his sword and delivered a powerful stroke that chopped through the buttonman's neck. The man's head tumbled across the floor and blood gushed from the stump of his neck.

"Rest well, my friend," the yakuza said softly. "You died with honor."

Without warning, one of the TRIO troopers fell forward and landed on his belly. A steel *shaken* was lodged in the base of his skull. Since the weapon was silent, only one TRIO goon noticed the fallen comrade. He turned swiftly, bracing the wire stock of his Beretta M-12 to his hip.

Rafael Encizo hurled another *shaken*. The throwing star struck the gunman squarely between the eyes. Steel pierced skull to the brain. The TRIO man's eyes rolled up toward the metal horn in the center of his forehead. Then he sank lifeless to the floor.

"*Wang-pu-tan!*" a Chinese gunman cursed as he turned to face the two Phoenix Force warriors who plunged through the doorway.

David McCarter fired the Ingram M-10 as he charged forward. Rafael Encizo unslung his H&K MP-5 and brought up the rear. The Chinese triggerman swung his Beretta blaster toward the pair. McCarter hosed him down with a lethal burst of 9mm parabellums. The guy's chest was chopped open and bullets tunneled into his heart and lungs.

The Chinese assassin fell in a twitching heap while the

Japanese swordsman desperately hurled his *katana* like a javelin. McCarter weaved out of the path of the hurtling sword. It struck the wall behind the Briton. Sharp steel sunk into plaster and the *katana* wobbled violently, embedded in the wall.

The yakuza had thrown the sword as a distraction more than a serious attack. He hoped the desperate technique would buy him a second or two, long enough to draw a 9mm Nambu pistol from his belt. The Japanese clawed for his side arm as Encizo opened fire with his MP-5. Three parabellum slugs blasted through the side of the yakuza's head and blew his skull apart. He collapsed beside the grisly corpse of the MERGE gunsel he had decapitated with the sword.

"Haaii!" a voice shouted as another TRIO killer attacked McCarter.

A red-oak club struck the Briton's Ingram, knocking the machine pistol from his fists. The Oriental swung a backhand sweep at McCarter's head. The British ace ducked under the club, but the assailant flicked his wrist and flogged the weapon across McCarter's back.

The *nunchaku* is a simple device, consisting of two sticks joined by a short cord or chain, and potentially lethal in the hands of someone skilled in the martial arts. The flexible weapon is very fast and deceptive. The sticks can strike with a hundred-mile-an-hour velocity that can break bones or rupture organs.

McCarter did not give his opponent an opportunity to continue the attack. He charged into the TRIO killer, ramming a shoulder into the man's gut. Both combatants crashed to the floor. McCarter pinned the thug and quickly stamped the heel of a palm to the guy's head, smashing his skull against the floor.

The Briton hit him again to make certain the goon was stunned before he wrenched the *nunchaku* from the man's grasp. McCarter quickly wrapped the weapon around his opponent's neck, drawing the chain across the hood's throat. He shoved the sticks hard, applying pressure. The Briton throttled him in a matter of seconds, crushing his windpipe.

The last TRIO hitman was the Chinese with the .38 Colt. He had managed to bolt for cover behind an overturned table. The gunman rose from his shelter and pointed his revolver at Encizo. The Cuban saw the assassin out of the corner of his eye. He dived to the floor as the .38 barked.

A lead missile jetted above the Phoenix warrior's tumbling body. Encizo rolled on a shoulder and landed on one knee, MP-5 aimed at his assailant. The Chinese gunsel shifted the Colt toward Encizo, but the Cuban's H&K machine pistol spoke first. It chattered out a 3-round burst of 115-grain projectiles that split open the TRIO man's face from mouth to forehead. The .38 Colt dropped from limp fingers as the Chinese buttonman slumped to the floor on his way to oblivion.

An armed figure appeared at the door to the auditorium. McCarter and Encizo turned to face the new arrival, weapons pointed at the entrance. They recognized the face of Gary Manning and quickly raised the gun barrels toward the ceiling.

"You guys okay?" the Canadian inquired.

"We're still in one piece," Encizo replied as he and McCarter rushed to the door. "And we'd like to get out of here before that condition changes."

"The others are checking the hall," Manning explained. "What's the local gossip on the Irish don and these other characters?"

"O'Malley is dead," McCarter answered. "Let's talk about these other blokes later."

"Hey," Encizo said. "I don't hear any shooting. Maybe the fighting is over for now."

"Maybe," Manning agreed. "But don't drop your guard until we're out of here."

11

Two squad cars pulled into the parking lot. Three San Francisco Police officers exited the vehicles. A fourth cop remained in a car, radio microphone in hand as he called headquarters for reinforcements. The three patrolmen jogged toward the O'Malley Enterprises building.

Two cops headed toward the furniture van and TV-repair truck while the third covered the door. An officer shuffled between the vehicles. Andrew Tanaka was waiting for him. The TRIO commander lashed out his *manrikigusari*. The weighted chain struck the cop's gun hand, yanking the service revolver from his grasp.

Tanaka slashed the chain across the policeman's face, smashing a weighted end against the cop's jawbone. The officer staggered into the side of the van as Tanaka swung the chain once more. The *manrikigusari* lashed a diagonal stroke across the officer's features. Blood squirted from his left eye socket as the chain mashed the eyeball to pulp. The cop opened his mouth and screamed, but his cry was terminated abruptly—along with his life.

Andrew Tanaka drew a *wakazashi* short sword from his belt and plunged the sharp steel blade into the officer's heart. His body twitched until Tanaka planted a foot in the cop's abdomen and pulled the sword from his flesh.

Another cop was about to circle around to the rear of

the van when he heard his brother in blue scream. The officer drew his service revolver and cautiously peered around the edge of the vehicle. He did not notice the passenger door to the van had opened a mere crack.

Harold Kuming pushed the door open and swung an arm like a catapult, hurling one of his steel exercise balls. The hard metal sphere smashed into the back of the patrolman's skull. The unexpected blow knocked the cop to his knees.

Before the cop could recover from the brain-rattling attack, Harold Kuming rushed forward and grabbed the officer's hair. The Chinese TRIO commander yanked back the cop's head to expose his neck. Kuming plunged the stiffened first and second fingers of his right hand into the center of the policeman's throat. The windpipe and Adam's apple were crushed by the deadly *chuan fa* technique.

"Pete? Joe?" the cop at the door to the building called softly, worried about the officers who had disappeared behind the van. "You guys okay?"

The policeman had heard a brief cry of pain, but he was not certain whether that meant one of his comrades had been killed. He had not heard any shots. Maybe somebody had caught Joe and Pete off guard and took them out silently. The cop figured that meant the bastards did not carry guns or they would have certainly used the firearms to deal with a couple of armed policemen.

The cop figured wrong. Andrew Tanaka aimed his Nambu 9mm pistol around the corner of the van and pumped two bullets into the cop's chest. Harold Kuming pulled the pin from a frag grenade and tossed it at the two squad cars. The officer who had remained at his vehicle was blasted into the night sky along with the cruisers. The explosion ignited gasoline, and fiery chunks of metal, upholstery and the dismembered policeman hurled in all directions.

"There will be more police here any minute now," Kuming told Tanaka. "Radio the rest of our men and order them to retreat immediately."

"More than half our assault force has failed to answer," Tanaka said grimly. "I knew we'd have some casualties, but I did not think there would be so many. The Irish don's defenses must have been far more formidable than we realized."

"What's done is done, my brother," Kuming said sharply. "But we must get out of here quickly."

Only a handful of TRIO agents survived to flee from O'Malley Enterprises. They dashed from the building and piled into the van. Two experienced thieves in the group tried to hot wire the TV-repair truck, but Phoenix Force had installed several security devices, including a double lock to the hood and a steel plate under the steering wheel to protect the wiring there.

TRIO solved the problem by jamming a quarter pound of plastic explosive under the dashboard of the truck. Then they fled in the van. A few seconds later, a blast ripped across the parking lot as the truck exploded.

"Son of a bitch," Gary Manning growled as he stepped from the O'Malley Enterprises building and discovered what had happened to the truck. "I should have booby-trapped both the truck and the enemy van."

"That wouldn't help us get out of here," James commented.

"But it sure as hell would have slowed down the enemy," the Canadian demolitions expert said. "Now they're gone and we're stuck here."

"Not really," Colonel Katzenelenbogen stated. "We've got the backup vehicle. We'll all just have to climb into the car and hope we can avoid any police roadblocks.''

''What if we get stopped?'' Rafael Encizo asked as he took the H&K MP-5 from his shoulder. ''If the cops catch us with all this automatic hardware, how do we explain it?''

''We have identification for Interpol and the Department of Justice,'' Katz reminded him. ''And we have federal permits for all our weaponry. We won't really get any trouble from the police, but they might take up quite a bit of our time, which is something we can't afford.''

''So let's get the hell out of here,'' McCarter suggested.

AMONG HIS OTHER ACCOMPLISHMENTS, Rafael Encizo was a talented photographer. Thanks to one of Calvin James's connections in the city, the Cuban was able to get access to a darkroom with no questions asked. The Cuban developed a roll of film and brought the photos to the Holiday Inn where the other members of Phoenix Force waited for him.

''I'm glad you remembered to take a camera on the probe,'' Katz remarked as the Cuban opened a manila envelope to remove the photos.

''I usually pack a miniature camera with an infrared lens just in case,'' Encizo explained. ''I took it on the probe because I thought we might need to photograph some documents or papers in O'Malley's office. Of course, that didn't happen.''

''What the hell,'' James said with a shrug. ''MERGE is definitely out of the picture now. Whoever these Oriental dudes are, they terminated the Irish don and his pals in the Colombian syndicate, Mexican mafia and Corsican syndicate.''

"David and I took care of a couple of those creeps," Encizo stated. "We didn't have much choice at the time. Point is, MERGE isn't the problem anymore. The mystery assault team is. That's what I took photographs of. David and I searched the corpses of some of the dead Orientals. Not surprisingly, we didn't find any identification papers, but David suggested checking for tattoos."

"You mentioned that before," James replied. "But you didn't explain why you figure these tattoos are important. I know certain gangs of convicts have a thing for tattoos, but I don't think these Asian guys belong to the Aryan Brotherhood—unless they've changed their rules for membership."

"Tattoos have always had special significance in the Orient," McCarter explained. "Not just decorations like the tattoo shops in Saigon. Tattoos are often considered living art objects and mystical symbols with magical powers. When I was stationed in Hong Kong, doing a little work for SAS, I learned a thing or two about how the tong operates."

"The tong?" James asked, frowning. "Chinese secret society of criminals, right?"

"Actually there are quite a few different tong societies," McCarter stated. "And most of them use some sort of tattoo as a unit crest."

"And we sure have some tattoos to show you," Encizo announced as he passed around the photographs. "Notice the black snake on the man's forearm? Three or four of the dead men had this same tattoo."

"All right," Katz began, examining the photo. "You're the expert. Is this a tong symbol?"

"I didn't say I was a bleedin' expert," McCarter replied. "But that's what I figure. Besides, I heard one of the blokes say *wang-pu-tan*. Now I don't know much

Chinese, but I do recognize that expression. It's 'bastard' in Mandarin.''

"Yeah," Encizo remarked, handing out more pictures. "But here's the odd part. Look at these."

"Holy shit," James muttered as he gazed down at an elaborate scene of bamboo stalks, with a sunset in the background and a large green serpent in the center. "This tattoo covers this dude's entire back. Don't tell me this is just a recognition symbol."

"It isn't tong, either," Gary Manning commented. "Last time I saw anything like this was when we were ambushed by those yakuza in Japan."

"That's what we figured, too," Encizo agreed. "Has anybody here ever heard of the yakuza and the tong teaming up?"

"None of us really know much about Oriental criminal organizations," Katz declared. "We'll need some help and I don't know where to find it."

"I think I do," Calvin James announced. "I know a fella who could probably help us—if he's still living in San Francisco. Guy's name is John Trent."

"Trent," Manning said as he wrinkled his brow. "The Justice man, Trumball, mentioned Trent. He rescued a couple of old ladies from some muggers."

"Sounds like the John Trent I know." James grinned. "Trent teaches martial arts. Used to instruct some of the San Francisco police in self-defense. John was born in Tokyo. His mother was Japanese and his father was some sort of diplomat who lived in the Orient. John spends most of his time in the Chinese and Japanese sections of the city. Since he speaks both languages fluently and understands the cultures and customs, he probably knows more about what goes on in Japantown and Chinatown than anyone else in Frisco."

"Would he know about criminal activity?" Manning asked.

"There were rumors in the police department," the black commando said. "Some folks figured Trent was connected with Oriental crooks involved in gambling and prostitution. John isn't always real cooperative. Cops tried to get him to help investigate petty shit before and Trent told them to get lost. He also tried to form a sort of vigilante group similar to the Guardian Angels. That didn't make him real popular with the police department or the mayor's office."

"Sounds like he's a bit mad," McCarter said, smiling. "I think we'll get along all right."

12

John Trent owned a *dojo*, martial-arts school, on Van Ness Avenue in Japantown. He remembered Calvin James and agreed to meet with the five men of Phoenix Force. Dressed in a loose-fitting black *gi*, Trent led the visitors to his office.

"Yi-Chyun Hai Shee," Trent said, examining the photographs. "The Black Serpent Society. Probably the second largest tong society in the world and certainly the most active here in San Francisco."

"You sound positive," Yakov Katzenelenbogen remarked. The Israeli wished he could smoke a cigarette, but the office was small and there was no ashtray, so he abstained.

"I am," Trent assured him. "I also read the morning newspaper. A 'gang of Orientals' apparently attacked O'Malley Enterprises last night. Poor Ian O'Malley was murdered, along with several business associates who were no doubt gangsters, as well. The papers depicted Mr. O'Malley as a generous and productive member of society. His security guards put up a noble battle, but they were slaughtered by the Yellow Peril. Great tragedy."

"You sound bitter, Mr. Trent," Gary Manning said. "I don't see why this upsets you."

"Maybe I'm just annoyed because everybody in San Francisco knew Ian O'Malley was a mobster, but now that he's dead they're ready to give him sainthood,"

Trent said with a shrug. "Maybe I don't like the implication of 'Oriental savagery.' I assure you, the tong is certainly no more savage than the Mafia and probably far more civilized than certain other criminal outfits."

"Then you don't think Oriental criminals are as bad as Caucasian crooks?" McCarter mused. "Careful, mate. Sounds a bit bigoted to me."

"I wouldn't say the tong is any better than the Mafia," Trent answered. "But I'm certain they wouldn't be any worse. So a bunch of gangsters killed each other last night. My sympathy goes out to innocent people and to brave individuals who protect themselves and others from the barbarians. I'm afraid I don't feel very sad about last night's 'slaughter.'"

"You don't object to the tong?" Katz inquired.

"No more than I object to any other form of organized crime," Trent answered simply. "Last night's raid is quite out of character for a tong society. They're generally far more discreet."

"Yeah?" Rafael Encizo raised his eyebrows. "Well, these fellas must not know the rules too well. They killed eight Coast Guard officers in order to smuggle heroin into the country. A couple of innocent bystanders were murdered when a car blew up a few nights ago. This isn't just crooks against crooks. And hoodlums aren't the only people getting hurt."

"Gentlemen," Trent said with a sigh, "you showed me some photographs and I identified the trademark of the Black Serpent tong. I don't know what else you want from me, but if you've heard that I'm associated with the tong somehow, then you've been misinformed."

"What about the yakuza?" Katz inquired, handing Trent another photograph.

"Yakuza?" Trent smiled thinly. "Well, I am part

Japanese so I suppose that might make more sense, but the yakuza keeps an even lower profile than the tong...."

"Look at the other photos," the Israeli urged. "Would you say those look like yakuza tattoos, Mr. Trent?"

"These are interesting," Trent stated, staring at the next set of pictures. "The tattoos are definitely Japanese, but that doesn't necessarily mean they're yakuza. However, they all feature serpents."

"Does that mean anything?" Encizo asked.

"It might mean these men belong to the Hebi Uji," Trent replied. "The Snake Clan. It is one of the largest yakuza networks in the world. One of the few that operate in the United States. If the Black Serpent Society and the Snake Clan have joined forces, that would indeed be a formidable combination."

"It was sure working well enough last night," McCarter commented. "Have you ever heard of the tong and yakuza working together before?"

"No," Trent replied. "But there is a first time for everything."

"How can we find out more about these groups, John?" James asked.

"You're not with the police anymore, are you?" Trent asked. "So who are you working for?"

"That's confidential, John," the black warrior told him. "Let's just say we're working for a bigger law-enforcement outfit."

"One that has a habit of bending rules in order to get results," Encizo added, sensing the independent maverick streak in John Trent's personality.

Trent smiled. His dark almond eyes seemed to sparkle. He leaned against the desk and returned the photographs to Katz.

"Oriental crime syndicates are like American chain stores," Trent announced. "If you want to find out what one of them is up to, ask the competition."

"You have someone in mind, Mr. Trent?" Katz inquired.

"Oh, yes," Trent said. "My uncle."

JOHN TRENT'S FATHER, Victor J. Trent, had met Reko Nakezuri during the reconstruction period in Japan after World War II. Most of Reko's family had perished during the mysterious firebombing in Tokyo that claimed more lives than the atomic bombs at Hiroshima and Nagasaki. Her brother Inoshiro had survived the war. A young officer in the Imperial Navy, he had been a cadet in training for combat when the emperor surrendered. Otherwise, Inoshiro would surely have died on the battlefield. Such an honorable death would have suited a man of Inoshiro's warrior nature.

However, the Nakezuri family were not descended of samurai blood. They had once been part of a clan of ninja espionage agents and assassins a hundred years ago. Inoshiro reluctantly accepted his sister's marriage to the American, Trent. The Occidental was a good man and he would treat Reko well, without denying her the culture and customs of her people. However, Inoshiro spoke little of his personal life and seldom associated with his sister and her husband until their son, John, was born.

Inoshiro had taken a deep personal interest in training his nephew in the impressive array of martial arts found in *nin-jutsu*. John became an adept student in karate, *ken-jutsu, atemi* and a dozen other forms of armed and unarmed fighting. When the Trent family moved to the United States, John feared he would never see his uncle again.

Then in 1974, Inoshiro arrived in America and took up residence in San Francisco's Japantown, only a few blocks from where John Trent ran his *dojo*. Inoshiro was operating, of all things, a television-repair store. This seemed a most curious choice of occupation for a shadow warrior and former Imperial officer.

John Trent had not been surprised when he discovered that the TV shop was a front for Inoshiro's true activities. His uncle was a sub-*obyan* chief for the Kaiju Clan of the yakuza. He was involved in black-market merchandise—watches, television sets and cameras. Inoshiro also dealt in fencing stolen merchandise, bootlegged videotapes and other relatively minor criminal activities.

Trent found his uncle at the TV shop. Inoshiro was always glad to see his nephew. The middle-aged Japanese had few friends, and he had never really mastered English. Inoshiro took Trent to the patio. A bamboo fence surrounded the area and a small wicker table was positioned near a rock garden with stones placed in Zen patterns. A young Japanese dressed in a white jacket with a compact automatic pistol on his hip brought tea for Inoshiro and his guest.

"My most favored nephew," Inoshiro said, sighing as he sipped his tea. "You have not visited me for weeks and now that you are here, you want to talk about criminals. Most unseemly, John."

"I realize you are a businessman, uncle," Trent said, smiling. "But your business is not entirely legal."

"Our ancestors broke the laws of the Japanese monarchs," Inoshiro replied proudly. "They studied forbidden martial arts, carried illegal weapons and fought to liberate the oppressed people of Japan. Would you call them gangsters, too?"

Trent realized his uncle's version of ninja activity was

somewhat different than how history records it. However, history is not always accurate. The ninja are usually regarded as sneaky murderers without the Code of Bushido of the samurai. In truth, ninja were very skilled and courageous and they also had a code of honor. Samurai occasionally raped and pillaged peasants. Even the worst critics of ninja never accused them of such conduct. Ninja never killed for sport or arrogantly decapitated peasants for failing to bow in their presence. They never resorted to torture or owned slaves. The same can not be said of the samurai.

Honor, like beauty, is in the eye of the beholder.

"Of course I would not criticize you or our honored ancestors," Trent assured Inoshiro. "After all, I, too, am ninja."

"Yes," Inoshiro said, nodding. "You are. A pity neither of us can practice our art. The world has changed, my nephew. I never would have become a yakuza in the old days."

"I know," Trent said. "And I know that your activities cause no one serious harm. The same is not true of the Snake Clan or the Black Serpent Society."

"You should not meddle in the affairs of these men, John," Inoshiro warned. "It could be very dangerous. Even for a ninja."

"The authorities are going to investigate the actions of these groups," Trent warned. "That means they will investigate other yakuza and tong networks. If the Snake Clan and the Black Serpents aren't stopped, your organization may suffer persecution and blame for the murders and narcotics traffic they indulge in."

"You cannot fight them alone," Inoshiro declared. "And I cannot turn against another yakuza clan. I hope you understand."

"I understand," Trent assured him. "And I don't intend to fight the gangsters alone—in fact, I don't intend to fight them at all.''

"I don't believe you, John," Inoshiro said. "You are ninja and you have an opportunity to use your art."

"If I decide to get involved I will keep my identity secret," Trent stated. "That's part of ninja traditions too. Please, my uncle. I need information."

"I cannot betray a confidence concerning a yakuza clan," Inoshiro replied. "But no code of honor denies me from speaking about a Chinese tong society."

"Do you know something about the Black Serpent tong?" Trent inquired.

"Not much," Inoshiro admitted. "But I'll tell you what I can. This is dangerous information, John. Be very careful how you use it."

13

Chinatown in San Francisco is the largest Oriental district found in a Western city. Twenty-four city blocks in diameter, it is twice the size of Japantown and much larger than New York City's Chinatown. Downtown Chinatown looks more like Hong Kong than Frisco. It features virtually hundreds of restaurants and openfront stores with signs printed in Chinese as well as English.

The color and excitement of Chinatown does not stop when the sun goes down. Neon and mercury lights are everywhere. Even the street lamps are shaped like pagodas. The traffic is always heavy, and the narrow streets are always teeming with pedestrians. Chinatown is one of the most fascinating spots in San Francisco.

The White Crane Restaurant was one of many exotic dining places located along Grant Avenue. It did not appear to be popular with tourists. When David McCarter and Rafael Encizo entered the White Crane, they did not see another Occidental in the restaurant. The establishment certainly would win no awards for charm or cleanliness, two qualities that are usually synonymous with Chinese dining.

The tables were circular with cheap plastic cloths and metal folding chairs. The floor was filthy, littered with cigarette butts and discarded wads of chewing gum. There was an obligatory bar with a mirror smeared by years of flyspecks. None of the customers were women, and they all looked mean. McCarter and Encizo moved to a table and sat down. Both men carried inexpensive AWOL bags and they wore loose-fitting Windbreakers that served to conceal pistols sheathed in shoulder leather.

A tired-looking Chinese with a toothpick dangling from the corner of his mouth approached the pair. He muttered something in Chinese that Encizo could not understand, but the Cuban did not need an interpreter to know what the guy meant when he jerked a thumb toward the door.

"Wei-mun bu-yau fan," McCarter told the Chinese. *"Wei-mun yau ching-bau. Dung-bu-dung?"*

"Your accent sucks, man," the Chinese growled.

"So let's just talk English and quit fuckin' around," McCarter replied, smoothly imitating a New York Queens' accent. "Okay, fella?"

"So you don't want to eat, but you want information." The Oriental shrugged. "What the hell you doin' here? This is a restaurant, not the Bureau of Information. And I already told you guys we're closed. Understand?"

"Hey, listen up," Encizo announced, adopting a Bogotá accent. "We don' need this shit, man. You go get your *jefe*, the boss, you know. Tell 'im we wanna make a deal."

"You wanta make a deal with the owner of a restaurant?" The Chinese snickered, but he glanced toward a group of Orientals seated at another table who were obviously eavesdropping with interest.

"Fock this restaurant," Encizo growled. "In Colombia we got pigpens cleaner than this dump. I wanna talk to your boss of the Black Serpents, no? Get 'im out here. We talk a deal."

"What are you guys?" the Chinese waiter said with a snort. "Cops?"

"We ain't cops, for crissake," McCarter muttered.

"Look, man," Encizo began. "The don is dead. Fock the don. We still gotta sell cocaine to somebody in the States. We don' give a shit if we sell to the Mafia or you Chinese guys. Is that clear enough, mister?"

"I think you assholes better get out of here," the waiter said tensely. "Or you might not be able to walk so good."

"Hey," McCarter said. "We're just messenger boys, you know. But you'd better tell your head honcho to consider our offer. You tong guys and your yakuza pals might have the heroin market wrapped up, but most popular powder on the block these days is cocaine. You'll find a hell of a lot more buyers for nose candy than horse. You're screwin' yourself outta one hell of a profit."

"Just a moment," one of the men at the other table announced. "We'd like to have a word with you, please."

He was tall for a Chinese, almost six feet, with broad shoulders and flat features against a chalky complexion. He was a man who spent little time in the daylight. Three other Orientals rose from their chairs as the nightcrawler approached Encizo and McCarter.

"You seem well informed, gentlemen," Nightcrawler remarked as he ran his fingertips along the lapel of his sports jacket. The leather strap of a shoulder holster peeked from beneath the gap. "How do you know so much about the Black Serpent tong?"

"All we know is they wiped out Ian O'Malley last night," Encizo replied. "That means they want his action, right? So we'll deal wit' 'em. Shit, man. We don' want no fockin' war. We wanta make money. Business is business and you don' make no money killin' each other. Right?"

"I make money by killing people," Nightcrawler said with a smile. "That's how I make my living."

"Just be sure you don't kill the goose that lays the cocaine eggs," McCarter told him as he leaned forward, covertly sliding his right hand toward the zipper of his Windbreaker. "Coke is worth its weight in gold, man. I don't think your boss would like it if you did something stupid that might cost him a couple hundred million a year."

"Really?" Nightcrawler chuckled. "But you two are just messengers, correct? I doubt if your lives mean much to anyone—including the Colombian syndicate."

Three men entered the White Crane Restaurant. Yakov Katzenelenbogen wore a pin-striped suit with a trench coat draped over his left arm. The prosthetic hook at the end of his right arm groped for the bar as he staggered into a stool.

"Had a few too many already, Fred," Gary Manning chuckled as he weaved unsteadily behind the Israeli.

Manning was also dressed in a suit and carried an attaché case. He slid onto a stool next to Katz while Calvin James leaned against the door, pushing it shut. The black man giggled as he slid a golf bag from his left shoulder and began poking about at the metal heads of the clubs.

"I want to show everybody the four iron that saved the day," James announced in a slurred voice. "Hole in one, man."

"I'm sorry, gentlemen," the waiter said as he rushed into the barroom. "We're closed for the evening."

"Closed?" Manning squinted as he stared at the waiter. "It ain't even ten o'clock yet. We just want a couple of drinks. Celebratin', you know."

"I lost this arm in the Korean War," Katz mumbled, holding up his steel hook. "Well, not this arm exactly.

It's artificial. But the one I had before it got shot off while I was fighting for my country.''

"You hear that?" Manning turned to the fat Chinese behind the bar. "This man is a war hero. Would you refuse to serve a disabled veteran?"

"I'm sorry, but you have to leave," the waiter insisted.

"I can't find my four iron," James complained, still searching in his golf bag. "Did one of you guys take it?"

"You were told to get out!" Nightcrawler snapped, angrily drawing a .38 Smith & Wesson revolver from shoulder leather. "Now, leave before—"

David McCarter swiftly drew his Browning Hi-Power and slammed the barrel across Nightcrawler's wrist. The weapon fell to the floor and McCarter swatted a backhand blow to the nightcrawler's face, striking the steel frame of his pistol against the creep's jaw.

"Freeze!" Enciso ordered, aiming his S&W Model 59 at the three goons with Nightcrawler.

"Nobody move," Katz added as he tossed off the trench coat to reveal the Uzi submachine gun.

"Good advice," James warned, drawing his S&W M-76 subgun from the golf bag.

Manning had popped open his briefcase and pointed an M-10 Ingram at the startled face of the Chinese waiter. Katz covered the bartender while James aimed his chopper at two guys at the end of the bar. McCarter shifted the Browning to his left hand and unzipped his AWOL bag to gather up an Ingram machine pistol.

"Everybody keep their hands up and move to the center of the room," Katz instructed. "Anybody gets cute and we'll have a bloodbath. If anybody doesn't understand English, I sure hope somebody translates for you."

"You can't do this," the waiter whined. "This is America. We have rights...."

"Well, if this ever gets to court you can tell a judge and jury about your rights," Manning replied.

"You scumbags murdered at least eight Coast Guard officers and four policemen," Encizo stated. "And you're trying to peddle heroin in San Francisco. That suggests you bastards don't give a shit about anybody's rights."

James herded the two men from the bar into the dining room.

"You, too," Katz told the bartender.

The man kept his hands high and nodded. He pressed the toe of his shoe on a button on the floor before he stepped from behind the bar.

"Okay," McCarter announced. "Now everybody face the wall and spread-eagle. After we relieve you of your weapons, we're going to have a little chat."

JOHN TRENT HAD INSISTED on accompanying Phoenix Force when they went to the White Crane Restaurant, which his uncle Inoshiro had described as an "NCO club for Black Serpent tong enforcers." However, Katz did not want to get a civilian involved so he insisted Trent remain outside as a lookout. Trent was given a transceiver and told to remain in the sedan parked across the street.

Trent was disappointed, but he reluctantly agreed to these terms. From the description of the plan Phoenix intended to use, it was not a job for a ninja, anyway. Trent was forced to admit that he did not have the experience and expertise of the men of Phoenix Force. He had never been in a firefight or fired a shot at a living target. Trent owned a shotgun and a .45 Colt pistol, but he did not have a permit to carry a gun. He felt like a rank amateur compared to Phoenix Force.

"Uh-oh," Trent whispered as he watched half a dozen hard-faced Orientals charge up the street toward the White Crane Restaurant.

Two men carried pump-action shotguns and another held a CAR-15 assault rifle. Trent figured all six men were armed and they damn sure were not Jehovah's Witnesses distributing copies of *The Watchtower*. Trent grabbed the transceiver and quickly pressed the On button.

The transceiver on Katz's belt buzzed. He automatically swung his Uzi toward the front door as he reached for the radio. The other members of Phoenix Force had disarmed the tong goons inside the restaurant and kept the hoodlums covered while their unit commander switched on the radio to receive.

"You're under attack," Trent's voice announced.

Two tong enforcers suddenly kicked open the door and dived across the threshold. Katz tracked the tumbling figures and triggered his Uzi. One of the thugs cried out as a trio of 9mm rounds riddled his body. The luckless hoodlum thrashed on the filthy floor. Then his movement became merely a series of feeble twitches as death claimed another victim.

The other tong goon rolled to the cover of the bar as a Chinese gunman aimed his CAR-15 around the edge of the doorway and opened fire. A stream of 5.56mm slugs sliced above Katz's head. The Israeli ducked, ignoring the sound of bullets thudding into walls behind him. He resisted the urge to return fire and waited for the enemy to present a better target.

Calvin James moved behind Katz to help his partner. McCarter covered the eight captives while Encizo headed for the kitchen in case more assailants decided to enter through a back door. Manning moved to the kitchen doorway, prepared to back Encizo or the other

Phoenix Force members, depending on who needed help the most.

Another tong killer leaped through the door, firing his pump shotgun as he ran. Bursts of buckshot smashed into the bar, shattering the mirror and numerous bottles behind it. One of his comrades supplied cover fire from the doorway, triggering a long burst from his CAR-15.

They were good, but Phoenix Force was much better. Katz and James were ready for the tong goons. The Israeli stayed low, his Uzi trained on the door. He fired a 3-round burst, drilling the 9mm projectiles through the chest and face of the gunman stationed there. The guy fell back through the doorway, his CAR slipping from twitching fingers.

Calvin James followed the progress of the shotgunner through the front sight of his S&W M-76. The black hardass triggered his subgun. Parabellums slammed into the tong killer and pitched him backward into a wall. The hood slid to the floor, leaving bloodstains on the wall. He made a feeble attempt to work the pump action of his Winchester riot piece, but his life seeped away before he could complete this final action.

The man who had darted behind the bar suddenly rose up with a Government Issue 1911A1 pistol in both hands. He aimed the big Colt at Katz and prepared to squeeze the trigger. James's M-76 snarled, and three 9mm projectiles crashed into the side of the pistolman's head. His skull burst like a rotten cabbage, and his corpse fell from view behind the bar.

A blue ball smashed through a window. It hit the floor and rolled toward Calvin James. The black man immediately recognized the M-26 grenade and lunged for it, hoping to chuck the blaster back at his opponents before it exploded.

Without warning, a hard object struck James's upper arm and knocked him off balance. He landed heavily on his side and glared up at Katz, startled to realize the Israeli had hit him with the metal "forearm" of his prosthetic arm.

"Leave it!" Katz rasped, keeping his eyes and the aim of his Uzi trained on the door.

A tong killer armed with a shotgun dashed across the threshold. Katz nailed him with a volley of Uzi slugs before the bastard could use his 12-gauge blaster. The man collapsed as an arm, holding a .357 Magnum, poked through the remnants of the windowpane.

Katz rolled onto his back, bracing the Uzi with the hooks of his prosthesis. He triggered the subgun, firing the last rounds from the weapon's magazine. The window dissolved and another tong gunman tumbled over the sill. The Magnum fell from the dead man's fingers.

James glanced at the grenade. He noticed the spoon was still attached. The pin had not been pulled. The black man turned to Katz. The Israeli was busy swapping magazines to reload his Uzi.

"How did you know about the grenade?" James asked, stunned by what had occurred.

"We've used that trick ourselves," Katz replied. "They wouldn't have lobbed a live grenade in here because it might kill their own people. So it had to be a distraction for another attack."

"You sure saved my ass, man," James said. "Thanks."

"Just returning the favor," Katz assured him.

"My pleasure," James replied with a grin.

The eight unarmed captives figured the gun battle was a strong distraction. They would not get a better chance to jump their captors. Nightcrawler and his three companions decided to try to catch McCarter off guard. The tong enforcers suddenly rushed the Briton.

''Bloody idiots,'' McCarter rasped as he lowered the aim of his Ingram M-10 and squeezed the trigger.

The British warrior raked a volley of 9mm slugs across his attackers' legs. Two men went down immediately, shrieking in agony as they pawed at their bullet-shattered limbs. Nightcrawler and one of his comrades kept coming. McCarter raised the Ingram and shot the flunky's face off.

Nightcrawler threw himself onto the Briton. Both men crashed to the floor. Although the tong enforcer's right kneecap had been smashed by a parabellum slug and another bullet had torn through his left thigh muscle, Nightcrawler still had plenty of fight left. He raised his right hand and slashed the callused edge at McCarter's face.

The Briton shifted his head to avoid the attack. Nightcrawler's hand chopped the floor less than an inch from McCarter's left ear. McCarter slammed the steel frame of the Ingram into his opponent's shoulder, knocking Nightcrawler off his chest.

A foot lashed out and kicked the M-10 from the Briton's hand. One of the creeps from the bar had decided to join the fight. McCarter quickly lashed out his own leg and drove the steel toe of his shoe between the tong goon's legs. The man screamed as his testicles burst like popcorn balls. He clasped both hands to his crushed genitals and sank to his knees.

Nightcrawler grabbed for McCarter's neck. The Briton rammed an elbow to the guy's breastbone and slashed the side of his hand to Nightcrawler's mouth. The tong killer sprawled on his back, dazed by the Phoenix pro's counterattack. McCarter turned his attention back to the man he had kicked in the crotch. He braced himself on his shoulders and swung his foot into the side of the flunky's skull. The creep's head bounced as if trying to free itself of his neck. Then he fell on his face, unconscious.

A rock-hard hand chopped against McCarter's skull, just above the temple. If Nightcrawler had not been weakened, his *chuan fa* stroke would have put out the Briton's lights. Instead, the blow only served to piss Mc-Carter off. The Phoenix Force war machine furiously turned on his opponent and slammed his fist into Night-crawler's face.

"You've had it, bastard!" McCarter snarled as he climbed on top of Nightcrawler and clawed both hands into the tong killer's face.

His thumbs found the corners of Nightcrawler's eyes. The Chinese thug realized what was about to happen and raised his hands to strike out at McCarter. The Briton's thumbs stabbed deep, punching through Night-crawler's eyeballs into his brain. The tong died so fast he did not even have time to scream.

The bartender, the waiter and the other clown from the barroom had attacked the other members of Phoe-nix Force. Gary Manning turned to confront the bar-tender. A short, fat man, the bartender still carried a lot of muscle under his flab. He charged the Canadian, fingers arched as claws.

Manning was probably the least ruthless of the men of Phoenix Force. Reluctant to shoot an unarmed oppo-nent, Manning allowed the bartender to close in. Sud-denly, the Canadian sidestepped and batted the frame of his Ingram across the tong goon's forearm. He pivot-ed sharply and slashed his left hand at the bartender's neck.

But the fat man was faster than Manning had expect-ed. He ducked under the Canadian's arm and swung his own karate chop to Manning's abdomen. The bartender rammed the heel of his other hand under the Phoenix warrior's jaw and drove a punch to Manning's stomach.

Most men would be rendered senseless by such a combination of punishing blows. Manning's head rang and his torso ached, but he was still on his feet and ready to dish out some punishment in return.

The Canadian swung a solid left hook to the bartender's jaw and rammed the muzzle of his Ingram into the tong's solar plexus. The bartender grunted, but did not double up until Manning chopped the side of his hand into the nerve junction where the man's neck and shoulder connected. The blow doubled the Oriental like an elbow joint. Manning slammed a knee under the guy's chin, breaking his jaw and sending him to dreamland.

The waiter tried to grab Katz from behind. The Israeli barely glanced over his shoulder. Then he swung his prosthesis low. The steel hooks snapped like the jaws of an alligator, seizing the waiter's genitals. The man bellowed in agony as the metal talons bit into tender flesh. Katz yanked hard, ripping the thug's testicles open. The man clamped both hands to the bloodied patch between his legs.

"Sorry." Katz sighed, genuinely apologetic that he'd hurt the guy so badly. "But you startled me."

Then he knocked the waiter unconscious with a blow from the Uzi barrel.

The other tong troublemaker launched himself at Calvin James. The black badass saw the attacker coming and immediately launched a side kick at the guy's gut. The tong hood blocked the kick with a karate chop to James's ankle. The hoodlum's foot lashed out, knocking the M-76 subgun from James's grasp.

"Shit," James muttered as the Chinese killer swung a deadly chop for his throat.

The black warrior executed a "praying mantis" block and snared the bastard's arm. He snap-kicked the tong slob in the gut and yanked him forward to ram a knee to the same area. The Chinese doubled over, and James stepped forward to drive an elbow to his kidney.

The guy fell forward and landed on all fours. He was a game little bastard. The hood lashed out an "iron broom" at James's legs. The Phoenix pro jumped above his opponent's sweeping leg to avoid being tripped. The tong enforcer scrambled upright only to receive a hard left jab to the chin. James jabbed his fist again and hit the guy with a right cross. The Chinese went down hard and did not get up for more.

The transceiver on Katz's belt buzzed again. The Israeli clicked on the radio.

"More enemies just arrived," Trent's voice announced.

"Holy shit," Calvin James groaned, rolling his eyes toward the ceiling. "How many sons of bitches do we have to fight tonight?"

"Hang around and we'll find out," Katz replied with a shrug.

14

John Trent could not stand being a spectator any longer. He had sat in the sedan and watched the battle from outside the White Crane Restaurant. Of course, Trent had seen little of the actual fighting, but he had heard the roar of automatic weapons and the *kiai* shouts of martial-arts experts in combat.

He had been sorely tempted to assist Phoenix Force. Trent had already pulled on black gloves and opened the blue airline bag that contained the two-piece scarf and hood of a ninja. He had also packed a pair of *tonfa* and a steel fan. Feeble weapons against machine guns, but damn it, he was trained as a ninja.

When the second group of enemy reinforcements arrived in a long black limousine, Trent radioed Katz and promptly donned his ninja mask and hood. Oriental hoodlums climbed out of the car and headed for the restaurant as John Trent slipped from the sedan and jogged across the street, holding a *tonfa* in each fist.

The *tonfa* is a simple weapon, a thick stick roughly a foot and a half long with a wooden handle at one end. It had once been used only as a handle for a millstone until Okinawan martial-arts practitioners learned it could be effectively used as a weapon. "The Prosecutor," which is considered a "new" type of baton by police departments throughout America, is actually a variation of the *tonfa*.

Trent reached the limo undetected by the hoodlums

who were hurrying for the restaurant. Four thugs with guns drawn headed for the door while the fifth goon remained in the car.

Suddenly Trent was beside the limo. He quickly thrust a *tonfa* through the open window and hooked the handle around the driver's neck. The hood uttered a choking gasp as Trent yanked hard, pulling the guy's head out of the window. He hammered the other *tonfa* across the driver's skull and left him unconscious behind the wheel.

Trent dashed around the front of the limo and attacked the other hoodlums from the rear. They heard his furious *kiai* and turned to see his airborne body hurtling toward them. Trent's right leg was extended as he executed a flawless jump kick. His foot smashed into the face of a startled thug before the guy could see what hit him.

Trent landed on his feet as a hood with an Uzi subgun swung his weapon toward Trent. The ninja slammed a *tonfa* across the barrel of the Uzi, deflecting its aim downward. The gunman triggered his chatterbox and blasted a 3-round burst into the man Trent had kicked in the face.

The ninja punched the end of a *tonfa* into the gunman's solar plexus and jabbed a second stroke, stabbing the hard wood into the man's throat. His windpipe collapsed and the man dropped his Uzi and slumped to the floor to die.

Another hoodlum tried to use his Beretta M-12 machine pistol. He might have succeeded if Trent had not been so close. The ninja parried the Beretta with a rising block, using the shaft of a *tonfa* to shove the M-12 toward the ceiling. He jabbed the end of his other *tonfa* under the gunman's rib cage. The goon gasped breathlessly as Trent's arms swiftly executed a scissor-action attack. He chopped both *tonfa* across the man's right forearm, striking up and down at the same time. Bone cracked and the thug screamed as the Beretta slipped from useless fingers.

The last gunman recoiled from the ninja and stepped across the threshold of the restaurant. He aimed an old M-3A-1 submachine gun at Trent. Yakov Katzenelenbogen fired his Uzi first, drilling three 9mm rounds through the bastard's head before he could trigger the .45-caliber "grease gun."

The man with the broken arm hissed like a serpent and pulled a *tanto* knife from his belt with his left hand. Trent whirled one of his *tonfa*, spinning it in his fist by its handle. The hoodlum jerked back his knife to prevent the blade from being struck from his hand. But Trent's tactic had only been a feint, and the thug had responded exactly as Trent hoped he would.

The ninja held the other *tonfa* by its shaft. He thrust it forward and caught the hood's wrist with the Y formed by the *tonfa* handle. Trent shoved hard, driving the blade of the man's own knife under his throat. The thug opened his mouth and vomited blood, his *tanto* buried in the hollow of his throat.

"Trent?" Katz asked, ninety-eight percent sure who the man with the mask was, but wanting to be positive.

"Yes," Trent replied rather sheepishly. "I just couldn't sit and watch anymore."

"I always knew you were weird, John," Calvin James remarked. "But I never figured you'd be crazy enough to take on four guys with machine guns while you were only armed with two sticks."

"We'd better get out of here before the police show up," Katz declared. "Help us haul the survivors out of here."

"We can't put all these guys in that sedan," Gary Manning told him.

"As fate would have it," Trent said, smiling beneath his black scarf, "our adversaries were kind enough to supply another vehicle. A nice big black limousine."

"Great," James remarked. "We've got the most classy paddy wagon in the city."

"Well," McCarter said dryly. "Isn't that just ducky."

PHOENIX FORCE HAD PREVIOUSLY RENTED a warehouse on the outskirts of San Francisco. The team frequently tried to secure at least one safehouse during a mission. Warehouses were ideal for this purpose because they were large nondescript buildings that could be used to store weapons, spare automobiles and occasionally prisoners. Phoenix had not informed Agent Trumball about the safehouse. In fact, they had not been in touch with the Justice man since their first meeting. Phoenix Force and Stony Man Operations worked on a "need to know" basis. Trumball did not need to know what they were doing, so they did not intend to tell him.

Phoenix did not need the limo, either. Although several enemy troops had survived the battle at the White Crane Restaurant, Calvin James said only three were in good enough shape for interrogation. They used the sedan and a rented Mustang, their newest backup vehicle. The limo had never seriously been considered by anyone except Trent. It was too conspicuous, too easily remembered by witnesses and located by police.

They transported the captives to the warehouse. James had given the three hoods enough thorazine to keep them in slumberland until they arrived. Inside, James checked the heartbeat and blood pressure of the unconscious prisoners.

"These dudes are doing okay," the Phoenix Force medic announced. "I still don't like using scopolamine without a cardiograph."

"Scopolamine?" John Trent inquired.

"It's a truth serum," James explained. "The only reliable truth serum, much better than sodium pentathol. Only problem is it can be dangerous. If a man has a weak heart or you give him too large a dose, it can kill him."

"True," David McCarter remarked. "But you've never lost a patient, Cal."

"There's always a first time," James muttered.

"We'll have to question them in their native language," Katz stated. "Mr. Trent, I understand you speak both Chinese and Japanese."

"I was raised speaking both Japanese and English," Trent replied. "My Chinese isn't as good, but I speak both Mandarin and Cantonese as well as a smattering of Korean."

"Very good," Katz said. "Then you'll be our translator. Calvin, let's have a conversation with our guests."

"I sure hope they know something we don't," Manning commented. "The White Crane Restaurant was our last lead. If we don't get another one soon, we'll be back to square one."

They interrogated the prisoners one by one. James estimated the proper dose of scopolamine needed for each captive. Katz told Trent what to ask and Trent addressed the first thug in Chinese. The man replied slowly, speaking as if hypnotized.

"His name is Lin Hsin," Trent reported. "And he says he's from Hong Kong. He arrived on the black ship that was manned by a crew of Japanese sailors. As you suspected, their cargo was heroin, which was processed at an island factory in the Pacific. Lin also confessed that the black ship was confronted by the Coast Guard. There is no doubt now that they murdered the Coast Guard officers off the coast of California."

"Ask him about the Black Serpent Society and the

Snake Clan," Katz said. "Find out if he knows any details about this new syndicate."

Trent translated the questions into Chinese. Lin nodded weakly and muttered *"san shee."*

"That's odd," Trent remarked.

"What did he say?" Katz asked.

"He referred to 'three snakes,'" Trent explained. "Let me try to get some more explanations from him."

Trent spoke with Lin for several minutes. The hood uttered replies slowly, his head rolling from side to side in a groggy manner. However, Lin remained in the drug-induced trace and continued to answer questions.

"He claims to be a member of an organization called TRIO," Trent told Phoenix Force. "Apparently it is comprised of the tong, the yakuza and a group calling itself 'the New Horde,' a variation of the Golden Horde of Genghis Khan. Lin refers to this segment of TRIO as 'barbarian Mongolians,' but he also says the New Horde supplied them with the opium from a base in Turkey, which was then processed by the tong and transported here by the yakuza."

"Jesus," Gary Manning muttered. "Sounds like we've stumbled across an Oriental version of MERGE."

"And apparently they planned to do away with the Irish don and set up their own syndicate here in San Francisco," Katz added. "They probably assumed this would be relatively easy because the Mafia is still fragmented and weakened by the beating it suffered from the Executioner wars."

"Yeah," James said. "They don't know about MERGE or they'd realize they're spoiling for a fight with an international crime network that is just as big and bad as they are."

"What is MERGE?" Trent inquired.

"Never mind," Katz replied. "Right now TRIO is our main concern. Try to find out if Lin Hsin knows where there's another TRIO base, either the headquarters of the organization or the place they have the heroin stored.''

Trent spoke to the prisoner once again. Lin Hsin uttered a brief reply.

"He says the headquarters of TRIO is everywhere and nowhere," Trent explained.

"Is he trying to be cute?" Manning growled.

"People don't try to be cute under scopolamine," James stated. "Sounds to me like the actual headquarters must be mobile. It doesn't have any one place for home base."

"But they must have a local headquarters here in San Francisco," Katz insisted. "Try again, John."

Trent questioned the man again.

"The local headquarters is outside the city," Trent announced. "But Lin isn't certain where it is. However, he does know where the heroin is stored...at least where most of it is, unless TRIO has moved it. Supposedly it's in a secret basement compartment hidden under the floorboards of the Five Rings Dojo."

"Do you know where this *dojo* is?" Manning asked.

"Everybody connected with the instruction of martial arts is familiar with the Five Rings Dojo," Trent confirmed. "It's probably the most expensive martial-arts school in the city. Most of its clients are business executives from the financial district at Jackson Square. *Sensei* Yoshimitsu runs the place. He is highly respected for his skill as a swordsman, but is also known to be quite arrogant and rather mercenary. One of those fellows who claims to be descended of samurai ancestors and feels that makes him better than anyone else."

"All right," Katz began. "Let's question the other prisoners and cross-check information. If everything agrees, then I think we'll have that new lead Gary was talking about."

15

Yoshimitsu Ito oiled and cleaned the blade of his *katana*. He stroked the cloth lovingly along the flawless samurai steel. The sword had been the soul of his family for almost three hundred years, passed down from generation to generation. Yoshimitsu regarded himself as a superior aristocrat, a knight warrior with noble blood in his veins.

In other words, he was a stuck-up son of a bitch.

Yoshimitsu knelt on the tatami mats of his office as he carefully returned the *katana* to its scabbard. He placed the honored weapon on a sword stand beside his desk. The swordsman had no chairs in his office. He refused to pollute his environment with Western corruption. Of course, he had no objection to accepting American dollars, but business is business.

Wealth and power had been part of the samurai traditions. It was part of Yoshimitsu's birthright, denied him by the cruel karma of the twentieth century. Thus, Yoshimitsu had found another way of achieving the money and influence that he felt he was entitled to. He had agreed to cooperate with TRIO. Naturally, a proud samurai would only reluctantly join forces with lowly yakuza, but one must occasionally make sacrifices in a world gone mad.

And surely it was madness that men of noble birth could no longer inherit the reins of power, Yoshimitsu thought. Instead, he had to deal with TRIO in order to make his fortune.

The fact that he was storing almost six hundred kilos of heroin that would be sold to addicts who would commit the most ruthless crimes to afford their habit, did not bother Yoshimitsu. If lesser beings suffered and died in order for him to make a profit, that was their karma. Yoshimitsu could not be bothered with such trivial concerns.

The telephone, another Western invention that Yoshimitsu was willing to tolerate, rang on his desk. The samurai answered the phone in the customary manner of the Japanese.

"Moshi-moshi," Yoshimitsu said.

"We have problems, Yoshi-san," the voice of Andrew Tanaka announced. "One of our business investments folded last night."

"Most unfortunate, my friend," Yoshimitsu said grimly. "Do you suspect this may affect my business, as well?"

"That seems possible," Tanaka answered. "We suggest moving valuable materials to a safe place."

"Transporting cargo isn't part of our deal," Yoshimitsu declared. "I don't run a freight service. You'll have to send someone to collect your belongings."

"Naturally," Tanaka assured him. The TRIO commander found Yoshimitsu's arrogance annoying, but he had long ago accepted the fact he would have to work with a lot of people he did not like. "We'll send someone tomorrow evening."

Yoshimitsu was familiar with the clandestine nature of TRIO. Tomorrow evening actually meant tonight or even this afternoon. TRIO, like all professional criminal organizations, never spoke openly on a telephone. One can never be certain if a phone has a police or federal wiretap. Yoshimitsu regarded such covert intrigue with contempt. Open combat, man against man with cold steel and individual skill determining life or death, was the way of a samurai.

"Very well," he told Tanaka. "But bear in mind that I have upheld my end of our bargain. I will not be cheated."

"I understand," Tanaka replied, secretly amused by Yoshimitsu's pompous attitude. The fool believed an organization like TRIO could be intimidated by his reputation as a swordsman. "You shall be rewarded, my friend."

"See to it," Yoshimitsu informed him before he hung up. Tanaka might be a unit commander in TRIO, but he was not Yoshimitsu's master. The samurai would decide when he wished to terminate a conversation with such an underling. Tanaka had not even been born in Japan, let alone descended of noble samurai blood.

Yoshimitsu rose from his glass-topped desk. The stubby legs of the furniture were so short that the desk could have been mistaken for a coffee table. Yoshimitsu walked to the window and drew back its bamboo curtain to gaze out at the view of Pier 39. Hundreds of blue water boats were docked in the marinas, majestic ivory vessels for the pleasure of those fortunate enough to afford them.

Yoshimitsu liked to pretend the yachts all belonged to him. The personal fleet of a wealthy *daimyo*, or warlord. Perhaps this was a silly fantasy, but he enjoyed it anyway. After all, the rich and powerful always seem to spend their money on elaborate nonsense. He thought he might as well start thinking of such things in advance.

RAFAEL ENCIZO WATCHED YOSHIMITSU through the lenses of a Bushnell 8x30. The Cuban and Yakov Katzenelenbogen had rented a yacht that morning and sat on the deck, conducting surveillance on the Five Rings Dojo. Encizo lowered his binoculars.

"I sure hope they haven't already moved the heroin," he remarked. "Yoshimitsu looks pretty damn smug."

"According to Trent," Katz replied, "that's Yoshimitsu's usual expression."

"Do you think TRIO has had enough time to move the dope?" Encizo inquired.

"It's possible," the Israeli admitted. "But it seems unlikely, unless the heroin was transferred to a different location before last night's incident at the White Crane Restaurant. I doubt they would have been able to find out enough details and report them to whoever's in charge of TRIO here in San Francisco to order the dope to be moved before now. Six hundred kilos is a lot of heroin. Nobody is going to carry it out in his pocket. Besides, if the heroin is hidden under the floorboards of the *dojo*, I don't think they'll try to move it as long as there are students inside."

"Yeah," Encizo agreed. "Trent said a lot of the guys who attend the Five Rings Dojo are businessmen and lawyers. Nobody would want to haul out a bunch of suspicious packages in front of those kind of witnesses."

"TRIO probably won't do anything until after the *dojo* closes this evening," Katz sighed. "But you know how surveillance works. You start assuming what your opponent is going to do and you start getting careless. After a while you're not watching too carefully. Next thing you know, the fellows you were supposed to keep an eye on are gone."

"I know," Encizo said. "If we get overconfident we'll probably make mistakes. Surveillance is one of the more routine and less dangerous parts of this work, so we're more apt to take it lightly. You've warned us about this before, Yakov."

"I probably sound like a mother hen at times," Katz said with a shrug. "But I've been in this business a long time and I've made a lot of mistakes and I've seen a lot of mistakes made by others. Amateurs make errors because they lack experience. Professionals make mistakes because they take too much for granted."

"Don't worry about being a mother hen," the Cuban said. "I can speak for the others when I say we never take your advice for granted. Like you say, you've been in this business longer than we have and you're still alive. That means you've been doing something right."

"I've been lucky," Katz said with a grin. "I've had the privilege of working with the best."

The other members of Phoenix Force and John Trent took turns with surveillance duty. This allowed each man to get a couple of hours sleep. So much had happened since they arrived in San Francisco that the team had been eating sandwiches on the run and grabbing a brief nap whenever possible. Without proper rest a man can not function at peak level, and the survival of Phoenix Force might well depend on every man being at absolute top efficiency.

The view from the yacht was impressive. The Embarcadero is one of the best known and most popular sections of San Francisco. Located by the coast of San Francisco Bay, it offers a breathtaking view of what are probably the most famous of the city's landmarks—the fabulous Golden Gate Bridge and the majestic Transamerica Pyramid that dominates a skyline of skyscrapers.

But Phoenix Force was not at Pier 39 for sight-seeing. The sun gradually descended in the sky as Gary Manning consulted his watch.

"Six o'clock," he announced. "That's 1800 hours to you military types. Figure Yoshimitsu has closed up shop for the night?"

"Looks like it," Calvin James confirmed as he gazed at the Five Rings Dojo through a pair of binoculars. "All the lights in the front of the building are out and a Closed sign is in the window. I think all the students left, too."

"Most martial-arts instructors teach private lessons to individual students," Trent stated. "But I doubt that Yoshimitsu will do so tonight. Not if he still has the heroin in his *dojo*."

"By the way," Manning began as he turned to McCarter, "are you still teaching self-defense to those butlers?"

"I have to do something to pay the rent between missions," the Briton said with a shrug. "But I don't put in any overtime out of the goodness of my heart. If those blokes don't pay attention in class when I'm teaching them how to fight dirty, that's their problem."

"I didn't know you are a *sensei*," Trent said with surprise. "What style do you teach?"

"Sort of a combination of ju-jutsu, *wing-chuan* kung fu and East London street fighting," McCarter replied. "I call it 'survival.'"

"We have to make our move soon," Katz announced. "Now bear in mind three things. First: this is the Embarcadero. We don't want to harm any innocent bystanders and we don't want to attract the police if we can help it. All weapons should have silencers attached."

"You have one I can use for my .38?" McCarter asked with a grin, referring to a Smith & Wesson snub-nosed revolver he often carried as a backup piece.

"This isn't Hollywood, David," the Israeli replied dryly. "This is reality. All our backup weapons are small or medium-caliber pistols and we wouldn't want silencers on them—even on the guns that aren't revolvers. Naturally you wouldn't use a backup weapon unless it was an emergency, and no grenades unless absolutely necessary. These rules apply in a situation like this even more than usual.''

"Right," Manning said with a nod.

"Second point to remember," Katz continued. "We got the tip about the Five Rings Dojo from a thirdhand source. It's possible Lin Hsin was given false information about this place. Everybody in that building might be innocent. That means we can't harm anyone unless they start a fight. Even then, no deadly force unless there's no other way to deal with a confrontation.''

"Third point?" James inquired.

"Even if Yoshimitsu and some of the others are members of TRIO," Katz began, "there may be one or more innocent students inside. This means we could have innocent parties mixed among the wolves. Possibly a hostage situation, as well. Even if our opponents take the gloves off, we still have to act with restraint. Understood?''

"Understood," Encizo confirmed.

"John—" Katz turned to Trent "—we're aware that your ninja training and martial arts are very impressive. You certainly handled yourself well last night. However, as you were honest enough to admit, you haven't been trained to handle automatic weapons or explosives and although you have considerable skill, you lack experience.''

"Does that mean I have to stay here as a lookout again?" Trent asked, frowning.

"It means we won't give you an automatic weapon," the Israeli explained. "I'm sure you agree that a man must be trained to handle a weapon if he is to use it effectively in combat. However, you do know how to use a shotgun or a pistol. Calvin will loan you a spare .45 if you join us for the assault.''

"Thank you," Trent said with a firm nod. "I want to participate."

"One condition," Katz added. "You're not a professional and we are. You'll follow orders, and you'll stay behind the rest of us unless we tell you to do something else. Otherwise, you'll have to stay here."

"Agreed," Trent assured him. "I still want to go."

"All right," Katz confirmed. "Then let's get ready..."

"Heads up, fellas," James announced, still checking the Five Rings Dojo with his field glasses. "A truck just pulled into the alley. This could be the heroin express."

"Double time!" Katz told the team. "The numbers are coming down and we'd better step on it before time runs out."

16

Two men stayed in the cab of the box-shaped truck parked in the alley by the Five Rings Dojo. Four others emerged from the back of the vehicle and walked to a side entrance of the building. A Japanese dressed in a *gi* uniform opened the door to admit the four visitors.

Phoenix Force pulled up to the curb, half a block from the *dojo*. They had acquired a new vehicle, a Volkswagen Vanagon. They had abandoned the sedan and Mustang because both cars could be identified to the police. A sliding door at the side of the minibus opened and McCarter, Manning and Encizo emerged.

All three men were dressed in black and armed with machine pistols and pistols sheathed in special holsters designed to accommodate the sound suppressors attached to the muzzles. Each man also carried a Bio-Inoculator loaded with sleep darts. Katz and James followed, dressed in the same black-suit garments and armed with silencer-equipped subguns and pistols.

Trent brought up the rear. He was clad in traditional ninja uniform, dressed in black from the top of his hooded head to the tip of his split-toe *tabi* boots. Trent carried a silenced Colt Commander in should leather, with a *ninja-do* sword thrust in the *obi* sash around his narrow waist. The ninja sword was slightly shorter than a samurai *katana*, with a straight blade and a wide, square-shaped hand guard. He also held a *han-bo* staff in his fist. The traditional fighting stick of *nin-jutsu*, the *han-bo* is less than four feet long and made of rock maple painted black. Trent carried other ninja weapons in a pouch on his left hip and hidden within his night-suit.

McCarter, Manning and Encizo reached the mouth of the alley. The Briton peered cautiously around the corner. He noticed the door to the *dojo* open, and two men carrying canvas sacks on their shoulders stepped outside. McCarter turned to his companions and held up two fingers and pulled his hand toward his chest. The others nodded.

They waited for the metallic clatter of the door at the rear of the truck being opened. Then they made their move. McCarter entered the alley first. One man was still carrying his bag while the other placed his burden in the open back of the vehicle. The Briton snap-aimed and fired his Bio-Inoculator. The air gun hissed softly and a tranquilizer dart struck the first man in the chest. He fell back against the truck and yelped in pain. The other man turned to face McCarter as Encizo moved beside the Briton.

"Good night," Encizo whispered, aiming his B-I pistol at the second man's chest.

The Cuban pumped a sleep dart into the startled man's torso. The guy was a husky Chinese who looked as if he might have been a former stevedore in Shanghai. He grunted from the sting of the dart and reached for a snub revolver in his belt.

McCarter swiftly moved in and grabbed the man's forearm before he could draw the weapon. The Briton jabbed the muzzle of his B-I pistol into the guy's gut and stomped a boot heel on an instep to discourage the Chinese from throwing a kick. Encizo closed in and clipped the man on the chin with the butt of his Bio-Inoculator. The Chinese did not have any fight left to resist the thorazine injected by the sleep dart. He slumped to the ground beside his unconscious partner.

Manning joined his teammates in the alley as the driver of the truck honked the horn, no doubt hoping to alert his comrades inside the building. The Canadian figured the other guy in the cab with the driver would get out first. He dashed around the rear of the truck to find the passenger had just opened his door and emerged, gun in hand.

The Canadian pro fired his Bio-Inoculator. The gunman groaned and leaned heavily against the door, but he still tried to aim his pistol at Manning. The Phoenix survivalist ducked behind the truck as the guy fired a .25-caliber pocket piece. The little peashooter barked with a sound as feeble as the underpowered bullet that bounced off the side of the truck. The gunman staggered forward and fell on his face unconscious.

The driver opened his door and hopped out on the other side of the truck. A black shadow bolted toward him as he yanked a gun from his belt. Trent lashed out with the *han-bo*. The black stick was almost invisible in the dark alley. The guy did not realize what struck his wrist, breaking bone and forcing the pistol from his fist.

Trent whipped the *han-bo* against the hapless gunman's face, hitting him on the cheekbone. The ninja grabbed the stick in both hands, turned sideways and rammed the hard end into the man's solar plexus. The guy doubled up with a choking groan. Trent carefully clipped him behind the ear to render the man senseless.

Another goon emerged from the *dojo* with a sack over his shoulder, apparently unaware or unconcerned about either the honking truck horn or the report of the .25 auto. However, light from the doorway spilled into the alley and illuminated the figure of the ninja standing over his vanquished opponent.

The goon immediately tossed the bag to the ground and reached for a .380 pistol holstered at the small of his back. Trent stepped forward and twirled the *han-bo* like a baton. Hard wood slammed into the hoodlum's head. He fell back against a wall, but managed to draw his gun.

Trent's leg snaked out, stamping his foot on the man's wrist, grinding it against the wall. The goon's fingers opened and released the pistol. He snarled and thrust his hand at Trent's ribs, fingers rigid as the heads of a spear. Trent blocked the attack with the shaft of his *han-bo* and snapped the stick across the aggressor's forehead.

The guy wilted to the ground and passed out.

"Heroin," Encizo announced, slashing open one of the bags to find it stuffed with white powder. "No doubt about the target now."

"Let's take 'em," Katzenelenbogen said.

Another Chinese appeared at the door. He had obviously heard the fight in the alley and emerged with a .357 in his fist. Gary Manning had moved to the front of the truck on the passenger's side. He used the hood for a bench rest and aimed an Ingram M-10 at the Chinese trigger man.

"Drop it," the Canadian ordered.

The guy whirled, swinging his Magnum toward Manning. The Phoenix fighter did not give him a second chance to surrender. Manning fired his Ingram and pumped three 9mm slugs into the man's chest. The impact hurled the hoodlum back across the threshold into the *dojo*.

"Stay back, John," Calvin James ordered as he charged to the doorway, M-76 submachine gun in his fists.

Trent flattened his back against the wall, obeying the

instructions of Phoenix Force as he had promised. James rushed past him and glanced at Manning, who had moved around the front of the truck. The black man tilted his head toward the door. Manning nodded.

James dived through the doorway. Manning quickly drew closer and fired a volley through the opening, aiming at the ceiling. The tactic was meant to distract and disorient the opponents in the *dojo* long enough for James to get safely inside.

Men scrambled across the polished wooden floor of the *dojo*. Most were dressed in *gi* cotton uniforms and did not carry weapons. But a few were armed with machine pistols and automatic weapons. The rest were rushing to the walls, reaching for an assortment of Oriental weapons that hung there.

Calvin James adopted a prone position and aimed his S&W submachine gun at the closest opponent who was toting a gun. The black commando triggered his M-76. The weapon coughed harshly through its foot-long sound suppressor. Parabellum rounds slammed into the enemy gunman's torso and pitched him across the *dojo* to collide with a *kendo* practice dummy.

The guy dropped his Beretta M-12 and seized the dummy. He wrapped his arms around it, pressing his face against the face mask of the dummy. The gunman died in that position, embracing the stuffed figure as if it was his lover.

Another gunner with a CAR-15 assault rifle aimed his weapon at Calvin James. Gary Manning, still stationed at the doorway, opened fire with his M-10. A burst of Ingram slugs sent the buttonman tumbling across the floor of the *dojo*. His rifle skidded beyond reach, but that did not matter to the gunman. He was already dead.

McCarter, Katzenelenbogen and Encizo had moved

to the front of the building. The Briton pointed his Ingram at the front door and fired a 3-round burst into the lock. Bullets chewed splinters from the door frame and smashed the brass bolt. McCarter stood clear of the door as he extended a boot and kicked hard. The door swung open and a salvo of full-auto fire erupted from within the *dojo*.

Bullets sizzled through the doorway. Several rounds smashed into a Cutlass Supreme parked in front of the building. Copper-jacketed projectiles shattered glass from a passenger window and punched into the metal skin of the car door.

Katz trained his Uzi on a window near the door and triggered his subgun. The glass pane exploded from the hail of 9mm missiles. McCarter and Encizo hoped this tactic had distracted the enemy within as they poked the barrels of their weapons around the doorway. Both men saw a skinny Oriental armed with an H&K 33-A-2 rifle. Both men opened fire. Half a dozen 9mm slugs hacked the TRIO gunsel's chest to bits.

McCarter dived through the entrance while Encizo covered him from the door. A salvo of large-caliber, full-auto bullets ripped into the floorboards less than two feet from the Briton's tumbling form. Encizo turned toward the muzzle-flash of a weapon fired at the northeast corner of the room.

A Japanese gunman was lurking behind a body bag suspended from the ceiling by a thick chain. The guy held an M-3 subgun that was still spitting bullets—right into the ceiling. The M-3 is a .45-caliber, blow-back-action weapon that is notorious for being difficult to control. The Japanese had not been able to stop the "grease gun" from climbing, so he wound up firing the last rounds straight up.

Encizo aimed his H&K MP-5 and unleashed a spray

of 9mm slugs. The body bag swayed from the impact of three bullets. Sand bled from ripped canvas. The Japanese jumped back from the bag, startled but apparently unharmed. He fumbled for a spare magazine to reload his M-3. However, he had hopped into plain view of Calvin James. The black warrior nailed him with a volley of 9mm destruction. The gunman's body was kicked sideways by the force of the high-velocity slugs. He executed a rather clumsy cartwheel and landed in a bloody heap on a judo mat.

None of the remaining TRIO hoods in the *dojo* was armed with automatic weapons, but they had no intentions of surrender. A man armed with a *kama*—an Okinawan weapon that resembles a cross between a sickle and a tomahawk—attacked McCarter. The Briton fired his Ingram and cut a line of bullet holes in the man's torso from crotch to breastbone. The attacker crumpled to the floor, blood spilling from his butchered flesh.

A *yari* spear hurtled across the length of the *dojo* as Calvin James rose to his feet. The lance slammed into the floorboards where the black man had been only two seconds before.

Rafael Encizo entered the *dojo* while Katz moved to the doorway to cover him. The Cuban noticed an opponent reaching for a discarded CAR-15 rifle. Encizo pointed his MP-5 and blasted a trio of parabellums into the guy before he could gather up the rifle. The goon sprawled on his back, blood splashing the white jacket of his *gi*.

"Let's go," Gary Manning told John Trent, deciding the risk had been minimized enough for their ally to once again join the battle.

Trent had taken care of the unconscious hoods in the alley, binding their wrists and ankles with plastic riot cuffs and gagging them. He had eagerly awaited an opportunity to participate in the fight, and now Manning had given him the green light.

There was not much of a fight in progress when the pair entered the main section of the *dojo*. Most of the TRIO thugs were either dead or had fled through another door to escape the gun battle. Only three opponents remained alive in the martial-arts gym. Two of these men held their hands high in surrender. The third displayed his stupidity by attacking McCarter with a *bokken*, a practice sword made of hard wood.

"Haaii!" the swordsman cried as he charged toward McCarter.

"Bye!" the Briton shouted in reply, triggering his M-10 Ingram.

Nine millimeters sliced through the man's upper torso, bursting his heart and puncturing both lungs. The swordsman performed an almost graceful pirouette and slumped lifeless to the floor.

James and Encizo moved to the archway where many of the TRIO flunkies had retreated. McCarter and Katz crossed the room to join them. The Israeli commando veteran gestured with his prosthetic arm, pointing the steel hooks at Manning and Trent.

"Take care of those two," Katz ordered, pointing the metal "hand" at the pair of TRIO followers who decided to give up.

"Not again," Trent sighed, reaching for some riot cuffs hidden inside a pocket of his ninja outfit.

"Cheer up," Manning urged. "The sooner we get these guys hog-tied and gagged the sooner we can join the rest of the party for more fun and games."

17

Calvin James and Rafael Encizo peered around the archway. The next room was another gym, slightly smaller than the main *dojo*. A flight of wide stone steps led to the next story and there were three doors along the west wall of the second *dojo*. Their quarry had vanished, either upstairs or through one or more of those doors.

"Shit, man," James muttered. "Hide and seek with killers."

"Cal and Rafael, check downstairs," Katz instructed. "David and I will see what's upstairs. We're running out of time. The police will arrive any second now. Finding the rest of the heroin is more important than terminating a few small-fry henchmen at this point. Be nice if we could get another prisoner or two for questioning, but don't take any unnecessary risks trying to take any of these snakes alive."

"Don't worry about that," McCarter said with a wolfish grin.

The four fighting men rushed through the archway. Katz and McCarter charged up the stairs as James and Encizo moved to the trio of doors along the wall. The black warrior noticed a judo mat at the east wall. One corner was folded back to reveal an open trapdoor in the floor. James stepped closer and looked inside.

"Jackpot," he announced, gazing down at the stack of canvas bags piled inside the compartment. "Here's the rest of the stash. Man, look at this shit. Must be about four hundred pounds of horse in there.''

"Let's leave it for the police," Encizo suggested. "After all, we're not on opposite sides. We just do things differently than the cops do.''

"Yeah," James said, grinning. "We break all the rules.''

"So do our opponents," the Cuban said with a shrug. "The police can confiscate this heroin and carry out their own investigation. Maybe—''

A door opened and an arm extended from the gap with a .38 Charter Arms revolver in its fist. Encizo whirled and triggered a quick burst from his MP-5. The gunman tumbled lifelessly through the door, the unfired .38 still in his hand.

Another door burst open. James turned and raised his M-76. An opponent rushed forward and swung a *nunchaku*. The stick-and-chain weapon struck James's subgun with vicious force, ripping the Smith & Wesson chatterbox from his hands. The assailant snapped the *nunchaku* in a cross-body stroke, clubbing James across the triceps. The blow staggered the black man, sending him stumbling into the wall.

The man with the *nunchaku* was a compact Japanese dressed in a white *gi* with a black belt around his waist. He had not gotten the belt through the mail, James knew. The little guy was damn good with his weapon. James ducked under another *nunchaku* stroke. A club brushed the hair at the top of his head. Hardwood struck the wall with a solid thud. The Japanese immediately swung a diagonal stroke at James's face.

The black commando jumped clear of the attack. His opponent slashed at James's kneecap. The Phoenix pro quickly shifted his leg to avoid the crippling blow. His opponent smoothly struck again, swinging a round-house stroke at James's head.

Then Calvin changed tactics. He suddenly moved in, raised his left arm. The chain of the *nunchaku* caught him high on the rib cage. A club section whirled around to strike his left shoulder blade, but the speed and force of the blow was reduced to a mere sting. James quickly snapped his arm down, trapping the *nunchaku* under his armpit.

The Japanese swung a left-hand karate chop for the side of James's neck. The black man's right forearm blocked the attack. He punched the Oriental in the face and slammed the edge of his hand across the man's wrist. James did not give the other guy a chance to counterattack. He slammed an *empi* stroke to the point of his opponent's jaw. The Japanese fell heavily on his backside and sprawled senseless at Calvin's feet.

Rafael Encizo had not come to his partner's aid because he had problems of his own. Distracted by James's battle with the *nunchaku* man, the Cuban had been caught off guard by another stick-wielding opponent. A six-foot-long *bo* staff lashed out from a doorway and slammed across Encizo's forearms. The blow jarred the MP-5 from numb fingers as a grinning Japanese snapped the hardwood shaft into Encizo's chest.

The Cuban stumbled backward from the blow. He almost reached for the S&W Model 59 under his left arm, but realized his attacker would not give him enough time to draw the pistol. The Japanese thrust the *bo* staff like a lance, the tapered end aimed at Encizo's solar plexus. The Phoenix veteran sidestepped the deadly lunge and grabbed the oak staff in both fists. He pulled hard, jerking his opponent forward.

Encizo's right foot caught the Japanese at the square knot of his brown belt. The Cuban straightened his knee to send his assailant sailing overhead in an abrupt judo circle throw. The Japanese crashed to the floor, and Encizo scrambled after him, drawing his *tanto* knife.

The Oriental thug started to rise, but Encizo seized him from behind. He thrust the heavy steel blade of the *tanto* between his opponent's neck and collarbone, driving the point into the man's subclavian artery. Encizo jerked the haft of his knife as if working the stick shift of an automobile. Blood fountained from the wound. The Cuban pulled the blade free. His opponent had already gone into shock. A second or two later, he would be dead.

"Oh, God," Calvin James muttered when two more adversaries suddenly emerged from another room.

One man was armed with a pair of *tonfa*. The other held a *wakazashi* short sword. Both charged straight for the black commando. James grabbed the *nunchaku* from under his left arm and took a step toward the man with the *tonfa*. He did not want to get caught between the two enemy martial-arts experts. They would tear him apart if they could attack simultaneously from both sides.

He took the best defense and attacked the *tonfa* man, slashing a *nunchaku* stroke across the stick weapon in the dude's left hand. James snapped his wrist, snapping the *nunchaku* to smack the guy squarely in the mouth with the end of a hardwood stick.

James turned just in time to block a sword stroke from the other opponent. The *nunchaku* rang against the flat of the samurai blade, deflecting the *wakazashi*. The black fighter delivered a quick backhand sweep and cracked the swordsman across the bridge of the nose with a *nunchaku* club.

James launched himself at the *tonfa* man once more. He swung the *nunchaku* in a lightning-fast figure-eight pattern. His opponent tried to fend off the attack with his wooden weapons. The *nunchaku* bounced against a *tonfa*, but James raised his arm and struck again. A club section hit the TRIO goon on the crown of his skull. James pressed the attack and delivered another blow across the right temple. The *tonfa* man dropped his weapons and collapsed with a fractured skull.

The swordsman slashed his *wakazashi* at James's neck, hoping to decapitate him with a single stroke. The black man dodged the whistling steel and struck out with his *nunchaku*. The chain struck the TRIO man's blade, the free stick section revolving around the edge. James caught the club in his left hand, trapping the blade with the chain.

Before the swordsman could react, the Phoenix pro punted a side kick to his abdomen. James yanked hard, ripping the short sword from his opponent's grasp. He flipped a stunning *nunchaku* stroke to the man's face and quickly grabbed both sticks to ram one end of the *nunchaku* into the hood's solar plexus. The man's mouth hung open, stringy spittle dripping from his lips. He clutched his torso with both arms as he dropped to the floor and blacked out.

Another figure dressed in a white *gi* uniform literally dived from a doorway. Unarmed, he pitched himself into the *dojo* and pounced on Encizo's MP-5. The guy hit the floor and rolled, coming up with the machine pistol in his hands.

Three flat-nosed 115-grain bullets shattered his face and burned through his brain before opening up the back of his skull. He died before he could even hear the muffled reports of the shots that killed him.

Gary Manning and John Trent approached Encizo and James. The Canadian lowered his Ingram M-10.

Smoke curled from the muzzle of the silencer attached to the barrel.

"You guys didn't leave much for us to do," Manning remarked dryly.

"I'd say you did enough," Encizo replied, glancing down at the dead man who still held the Cuban's gun in his fists.

Katz and McCarter had also been busy staying alive. Before they climbed halfway up the stairs to the next story, a figure appeared at the head of the stairs. The TRIO enforcer aimed a Beretta M-12 at the Phoenix pair. Katz braced his Uzi across his prosthesis, barrel pointed upward. He squeezed the trigger.

The Uzi uttered three rapid coughs through its sound suppressor. The gunman at the head of the stairs screamed as 9mm slugs crashed into his body. He fell backward, firing his Beretta blast machine at the ceiling. Chunks of plaster and loose dust showered down on Katz and McCarter.

"Aiiee!" a voice echoed through the stairwell.

It belonged to a Japanese American who leaped from the head of the stairs, armed only with a pair of *sai*. He landed feetfirst on the same riser that Katz was standing on and struck out with both *sai*.

The *sai* is an Okinawan weapon, similar to a short sword with a long center blade and a curved prong extending from each side. The attacker's right-hand *sai* snared the barrel of Katz's Uzi, trapping it between center blade and prong. He thrust the other *sai* at the Israeli's ribs, hoping to drive the point into Katz's heart.

The Phoenix Force commander's prosthesis blocked the attack. The steel hooks at the end of his artificial arm snapped shut around the center blade, holding the weapon at bay. Katz did not intend to waste time struggling with his opponent. He promptly butted the front of his skull against the Oriental's face, breaking the bridge of the man's nose.

Katz pumped a knee between his opponent's legs. The man gasped in pain and started to double over. The Israeli abruptly twisted his body to the left and pushed the TRIO man off balance. The Japanese tumbled down the stairs to land against the stone steps in a battered, senseless lump.

Suddenly McCarter pressed his left hand against Katz's back, shoving the Israeli into the handrail. The British ace raised the Ingram M-10 in his right fist and fired a salvo at another TRIO buttonman who appeared at the head of the stairs.

Firing the machine pistol one-handed reduced accuracy. Three 9mm slugs slammed into the enemy gunman's upper torso and left shoulder. The sledgehammer force of the bullets spun the man like a top, although he still held on to his MAT-49 submachine gun. McCarter sprayed him with another burst of parabellum rounds. The man's spinal cord snapped like a thread. His corpse toppled forward. McCarter and Katz stepped aside as the dead man rolled down the stairs.

The two Phoenix Force commandos continued up the stairs. They discovered a deserted corridor with four doors. They watched the hallway, weapons held ready, and waited for their teammates to arrive. Manning and John Trent soon mounted the stairs to assist.

"Everybody all right down there?" Katz inquired.

"Yeah," Manning assured him. "A few of the bad guys won't get up again, but Rafael and Cal are okay. They managed to take two of the bastards alive—more or less. Figured they could bind and gag their own prisoners."

"Cover us," the Israeli instructed. "Watch the other

doors while David and I check out the rooms one by one."

They carried out the search professionally, standing clear of each door as they kicked it open. The Phoenix pros inspected each room quickly, but efficiently. The first three rooms contained no hidden opponents. Only the office of Yoshimitsu Ito remained.

McCarter opened the door with a firm kick. Katz entered, Uzi barrel first. The *sensei*'s office was spacious, but contained little furniture. Certainly nothing that Yoshimitsu could hide behind. There was no sign of the owner of the Five Rings Dojo. An open window suggested where Yoshimitsu had gone.

"Looks like the captain decided to abandon ship," McCarter mused aloud as he walked to the window and cautiously examined the fire escape just in case Yoshimitsu was still lurking there. He was not.

"Pity," Katz sighed. "Yoshimitsu would probably be the best man to question about TRIO's headquarters."

"Well," Manning began as he and Trent entered the office, "one of the bigger fish got away, but we did locate the cache of heroin. At least TRIO won't be peddling any more dope for a while."

"A very short while," Katz replied. "We've only hacked off a few tentacles. The head of the octopus remains intact."

"Yoshimitsu took his *katana*," Trent remarked, noticing the sword stand was empty. "I'm certain he intends to use it on us in the future."

"Too bad he didn't hang around to try now," McCarter said.

"We can't afford to hang around any longer, either," Katz announced. "Let's get out of here."

18

"I wish to remind you gentlemen about the law concerning kidnapping," one of the captives declared the moment the gag was removed from his mouth. "There's a common misconception that the Lindbergh ruling means kidnapping is automatically a capital offense. Actually, this is only true if you hold an individual for ransom...."

"This guy's gotta be a lawyer," Calvin James remarked. "What are you, fella? Yoshimitsu's mouthpiece?"

"My name is Donald Hirto," the Japanese American announced. "As a matter of fact, I am an attorney-at-law. And you'd best listen to me before you do anything that might get you in worse trouble than you are already—"

"I hate to disillusion you, amigo," Rafael Encizo said with a grin, "but you're in a worse position than we are right now, in case you didn't notice."

Phoenix Force had only taken four captives from the Five Rings Dojo. They selected one of the Chinese hoods who had arrived in the truck to transport the heroin, the two men who had willingly surrendered and the Japanese *nunchaku* expert. Phoenix loaded the prisoners into the minibus and took them to the safehouse.

"Who are you men?" Hirto demanded. "Gangsters? Terrorists? Some sort of neo-Nazi organization?"

"We're the guys who you'd better talk to if you have any long-term ambitions in life," Katzenelenbogen replied as he sat on a crate across from Hirto and lighted a Camel cigarette. "Such as seeing the sun come up in the morning."

"You can't threaten me!" the lawyer snapped. "And any confession you might be able to beat out of me would not be admissible in court."

"Do you have something to confess to, Hirto?" Katz inquired, raising his eyebrows.

"I'm just an attorney," Hirto said, shifting uncomfortably in the chair he was securely bound to. "I don't know why you kidnapped me...."

"You haven't been kidnapped," the Israeli informed him. "You're a prisoner of war. Of course, this is sort of an undeclared war. No diplomats or politicians involved. No Geneva Convention. I hope you're not foolish enough to just give us 'name, rank and serial number.'"

"We're not playing games with you blokes," David McCarter told Hirto. "You'd better tell us everything you know about TRIO."

"TRIO?" Hirto said with a nervous smile. "Look, gentlemen, I'm just one of many lawyers and businessmen who studied kendo under *Sensei* Yoshimitsu. That's a common practice in Japan, you know. Sword fighting builds spiritual strength and helps you focus aggression on goals rather than senseless anger. It's also a fine way to release frustrations, swinging away with a bamboo sword..."

"Just an innocent student who suddenly found himself in the middle of a shooting spree, eh?" Encizo remarked. "You had no idea Yoshimitsu was involved in anything illegal, is that it?"

"Yes," Hirto confirmed. "That's right...."

"You expect us to believe that TRIO would transfer the heroin right in front of you?" Encizo asked. "They didn't figure somebody would get suspicious when they saw men hauling sacks of powder from a secret compartment in the floor to the truck waiting in the alley outside?"

"I assumed the sacks contained sand or rice," Hirto stated. "How should I know what was inside those bags?"

"There were men armed with automatic weapons in the main *dojo*," Calvin James commented. "What did you think that was for? A twenty-one-gun salute for a military funeral?"

"Mr. Hirto," Katz began, "as a lawyer, you must be aware that if an individual gives information willingly, he can often avoid facing charges for involvement in organized crime. If you're a state's witness you'll certainly be granted immunity. You'll be placed in protective custody and probably relocated somewhere else in the country under a new name."

"The hell with this crap," McCarter snapped. "Let's beat some answers out of this smug little bastard."

"Take it easy, man," James urged. "Let me give this dude a physical and figure out how much scopolamine to use on him."

"Wait a minute," Hirto insisted. "If you men are police or government agents, you can't use these sorts of tactics—kidnapping, threats, truth serum. Then again, you can't legally burst into an establishment without a search warrant and not bother to announce that you're law-enforcement personnel and show proper ID. You're operating outside the law. You can't turn me over to the police because you're criminals yourselves. If I talk, how do I know you won't kill me?"

"We can't exactly explain what we are," Katz said.

"But we're not with the police or directly associated with the government. You see, law-enforcement agencies must follow laws and guidelines. However, there are certain types of criminals who are too slippery to catch if one follows the law to the letter. We only handle jobs where we can throw the rule book out the window. We don't pride ourselves on savagery or ruthlessness. We're professionals, and professionals have to follow certain codes of honor and integrity or they're no better than savages."

"I don't understand," Hirto admitted.

"I wouldn't expect you to understand honor," Katz replied simply. "You're an attorney, but you probably don't understand justice, either. To you the law is only a tool for ambitions. Twist and tear the law apart for the sake of your clients, but never worry about justice. Right? I doubt if you could ever understand something like honor."

"All you need to know is things will go better for you if you cooperate with us," Encizo told Hirto. "Now, we had three Chinese tong members who we questioned under scopolamine earlier. We just kept them doped up and dropped them off in a park and called the police. An anonymous tip told the cops where to pick the guys up. We can do the same thing with you or you can be a state's witness and not have to take the fall when TRIO comes tumbling down."

"You don't understand TRIO," Hirto declared. "You can't beat them. It's like fighting your shadow. Even if you beat them here in San Francisco, they'll be back. You have no idea how big TRIO is, how powerful and cunning. They have their own ideas about honor, too. Have you ever heard of a member of a Chinese tong or a yakuza clan testifying against his organization? Never. They never betray their brotherhood, and they'd never stop hunting for me if I betrayed them now."

"Have it your way, Mr. Hirto," Katz responded. "But you'll talk under the influence of the scopolamine. TRIO will probably consider you a traitor either way."

"Either way—" Hirto shook his head with dismay "—I lose, don't I? Very well, I guess the only chance I've got is to hope protective custody can keep me alive for a year or two."

"I'll get the tape recorder," Gary Manning announced. "You can make a full confession on tape. Then we'll drop you off about a block from a police station. The tape will be our insurance that you'll turn yourself in."

"I thought you fellas were smart." Hirto smiled bitterly. "I'll make the confession on tape, but it won't be admissible in court, either. You can't blackmail me that way."

"Who said anything about giving the tape to the police?" Encizo inquired. "No, Hirto, we wouldn't do that. But if you don't turn yourself over to the cops, we'll find a way to get the tape to TRIO instead."

"You bastards," Hirto said. "You'd do it, too. What if I refuse? Then you'd just record my answers while I'm under the influence of truth serum, I suppose."

"Thanks for the idea." Encizo smiled. "Look, we don't have all night, Hirto."

"Get the recorder," the lawyer said grimly. "I'll cooperate, but do me a favor: no more lectures about honor. You jokers play just as dirty as the gangsters."

"We don't peddle heroin or murder innocent people," Katz replied. "But I don't feel like arguing with you. Make your confession and we'll keep our end of the deal."

"Wonderful," Hirto muttered sourly as Gary Manning handed him a tape recorder. "Christ, I wish I'd never gotten involved in this mess."

"In other words," Encizo said, "you wish you hadn't got caught. Turn on the machine and let's hear the story of your life. Just edit out everything that isn't connected with TRIO."

Donald Hirto explained that he had become involved with TRIO when he became a legal adviser to the San Francisco section of the yakuza Snake Clan. Hirto was basically a contract lawyer, hired to help the Japanese gangsters invest money into new ventures and acquire control of new businesses.

TRIO wanted to expand, and they hired Hirto to help them. Among his other duties, Hirto was to help with tax loopholes and business deductions to keep the IRS from probing too deeply into TRIO-related operations. One of these tricks included a phony Buddhist temple located in the Marin Peninsula.

Suddenly Encizo switched off the tape recorder.

"What's the matter?" Hirto asked, bewildered by the Cuban's actions.

"I don't want my voice recorded on the tape," Encizo explained. "But I have a question. Why would TRIO want this fake temple? The tax-shelter angle doesn't explain it. Why establish a bogus temple just to contribute to it and recycle your own money? Simpler just to keep the cash or invest in something else."

"You have a theory about this temple?" Katz inquired.

"Remember Lin Hsin?" the Cuban asked. "The Chinese hoodlum who told us the headquarters for TRIO was located outside of San Francisco? This Buddhist temple is in Marin Peninsula, right? Is it located in a remote area?"

"In a forest," Hirto answered. "Not exactly Death Valley, but several miles from its nearest neighbors."

"Is this temple a large building?" Gary Manning asked the lawyer.

"I've never been there," Hirto stated. "But I assume it is a relatively large building. The forest is private property, also owned by the Green Hat Buddhist sect, which is a TRIO front."

"A mysterious religious cult," Manning mused. "That wouldn't seem unusual in California. If it didn't try to recruit middle-class white kids or panhandle in airports, nobody would even be curious about it."

"Could be TRIO's headquarters in this area," Katz stated. "Turn on the recorder so Hirto can continue his confession. But, Mr. Hirto, don't mention the temple."

"You don't want the police to know about it?" Hirto inquired.

"I have a feeling they'll already know about it by the time they hear the tape," Katz told him. "And it may be better for you if the authorities don't associate you with it."

"What do you gentlemen plan to do?" Hirto asked.

"I don't think you really want to know," Katz replied.

"Not so sure I want to know, either," Calvin James added with a sigh.

19

The steel exercise balls clicked again and again as Harold Kuming worked the metal spheres in his right hand, fingers moving like the antennae of a frustrated insect. The Chinese American unit commander for TRIO paced the floor while Andrew Tanaka and Yoshimitsu Ito conversed in Japanese. The three men had congregated in a small office at the Green Hat Buddhist temple. The meeting was not a happy one.

"Yoshi-san has explained what happened at his *dojo*," Tanaka told Kuming. "Whoever attacked his school did so with total ruthlessness and savage fury. They entered with guns blazing, armed with full-auto weapons."

"The same men who struck at the White Crane Restaurant," Kuming commented. "But who are they?"

"Yoshi-san does not know," Tanaka answered. "He was most fortunate to escape with his life."

"Personally, I would rather Yoshi-san lost his life instead of the heroin he was supposed to be protecting," Kuming said with a sneer. "I thought samurai were supposed to commit hara-kiri when they've failed to carry out their duties."

"Those Chinese dogs you sent to transport the heroin failed, not I!" Yoshimitsu snapped as he rose to his feet, right hand gripping the haft of his *katana*. "And the proper name for ritual suicide is *seppuku*, not hara-kiri, you ignorant half-breed."

"Please, let's not argue among ourselves," Tanaka urged. "This is no time for disputes or insults. Nor do we have time to waste blaming each other for the loss of the heroin. There will be time for that later."

"Your point is well taken, my brother." Kuming was forced to agree as he walked to a four-foot-high ceramic urn with a red dragon painted across its white surface. "For now we must concentrate on action. Our first concern is to maintain the security of TRIO. Unfortunately it is too late to salvage our operations in San Francisco. We'll have to move our people out of the city as quickly as possible and set up elsewhere."

"The Emperors of TRIO will be most distressed." Tanaka frowned. "Our organization has never suffered such a great setback before. Some of us will pay dearly for this failure."

"Some sooner than others," Kuming added.

He suddenly shouted a battle cry and drove the tips of his powerful fingers into the urn. Porcelain burst and a long crack appeared in the urn. Kuming shoved hard and the urn split. A large chunk of thick porcelain crashed to the floor. Kuming turned to Yoshimitsu.

"After we've taken care of essential business," the Chinese American announced, "you and I will settle our personal quarrel."

"With pleasure," Yoshimitsu replied, nodding in agreement.

THE FIVE MEN OF PHOENIX FORCE and John Trent crept through the forest, moving from tree to tree. The trees blotted out the night sky, and little starlight peeked through the ceiling of leaves. However, their eyes had adjusted well to the darkness. To further ensure efficiency in the dark, Encizo and Katz wore infrared goggles that reduced the shadows of night to mere dusk.

Gary Manning also carried a Starlite viewer that served as an effective telescope even in the blackest night.

All six men were clad in black. Trent wore his ninja night suit, armed with his *ninja-do* sword and the .45 Colt Commander. He had also carried an assortment of other *nin-jutsu* gear in a pouch on his hip and a black backpack between his shoulder blades.

McCarter, Katz and Encizo carried the same weapons they had favored throughout the mission, with the addition of more grenades, knives and garrotes. Manning had exchanged his M-10 for an FLN assault rifle with an infrared scope, and Calvin James had selected an M-16 assault rifle with an M-203 grenade launcher attached to the barrel beneath the muzzle.

"The temple is up ahead," Manning announced, gazing through his Starlite viewer. "About two hundred meters."

"I see it," Encizo added. "Doesn't look very holy to me. Or very friendly."

The temple was a pagodalike structure with graceful sloped roofs of red tile. It was three stories tall with a watchtower garret and wooden balconies. Sentries armed with CAR-15 rifles patrolled the grounds. Guards were also stationed along the catwalks of the balconies.

"I count six sentries," Katz declared. "Two outside, two on the first-story porch walkway and one on each level above."

"Wish I had my crossbow," McCarter whispered. "I guess Gary and Cal will have to take care of the chaps on the top two stories."

"Right," Katz confirmed. "Let John take a look at the temple through the Starlite, Gary."

The Canadian handed his night viewer to Trent. The ninja looked through the Starlite and nodded at Katz.

"I can climb it, Colonel," he assured the Israeli.

"All right," Katz replied. "I see a truck and at least four cars parked by the temple. Better expect quite a few of the enemy to be inside. Gary, you and Cal know what to do. David and Rafael will take the men on the porch. John and I will handle the foot patrol outside. Remember we'll be attacking from three different directions. Be careful not to hit one of our own."

"What about prisoners?" Manning inquired.

"That'll be up to TRIO," the Israeli replied. "We're not murderers, but I don't think any of these fellows are going to surrender. Any survivors should be bound and left behind. We're not taking any captives with us this time. Whether we win or not, this will be the final battle of this mission. Now let's get in position."

Manning and James attached foot-long sound suppressors to the threaded muzzles of their rifles. Both men aimed carefully, peering through the infrared scopes. The cross hairs of James's night scope found the face of the second-story sentry.

James triggered his weapon. Three rounds sputtered from the silencer. A trio of 5.56mm projectiles splintered the bridge of the sentry's nose and punched through his right eyebrow. The man's eyeball popped out of its cracked socket, swinging from the thick stem of an optic nerve.

Manning, the best marksman of Phoenix Force, opened fire a split second later. He placed a single 7.62mm slug through the side of his target's head. The man on the third-story balcony twisted when the bullet crashed through his temple into his brain. He slumped to the catwalk, as dead as a rusty coffin nail.

John Trent suddenly charged from the tree line. A startled sentry turned sharply when he heard the hiss of a subdued *kiai*. The last thing he saw in his life was the flash of a steel ribbon as he tried to raise his CAR-15. Trent's sword struck the man in the crown of the head and sliced through skull and brain matter to the bridge of his nose. Trent then thrust the slanted point of his *ninja-do* through the heart of his opponent.

The other guard who patrolled the grounds, saw the mysterious black figure strike down his comrade. The sentry swung his rifle toward Trent, but something clamped around his wrist like the beak of a killer eagle. The grip crushed bone as if it were dry leaves. The sentry opened his mouth to scream, but a gloved hand smothered his lower face to silence his cry.

Yakov Katzenelenbogen stamped a boot into the back of his opponent's knee and pulled the man to the ground. The Israeli's steel hooks released the sentry's crushed wrist and descended upon the guard's throat. Katz worked the prosthesis, tightening the metal talons into the man's windpipe and carotid arteries. Within seconds, the Phoenix Force commander throttled him to death.

Encizo and McCarter acted simultaneously as they rushed toward the temple. The two sentries on the porch walkway fumbled with their weapons, astonished that two shadows of the night had materialized into armed aggressors. The British and Cuban commandos fired their machine pistols. The silenced weapons rasped death. Both sentries toppled to the walkway, bloodstains blossoming on their shirts.

Trent moved to a corner of the building and quickly removed his backpack. The ninja removed a pair of *ashiko* spiked bands and tied them to his feet, fastening the ropes around the instep and across the split-toe of his *tabi* foot gear. Next, Trent strapped a pair of similar spiked bands around his hands. He draped a coil of nylon rope around his shoulder and grasped the wall, digging in with the points of the *shuko* claws at the palms of his hands. He hauled himself up and dug the *ashiko* spikes into the wall.

He repeated this over and over, scaling the stone surface like a squirrel. Trent reached the third story and grabbed a wooden rail to a balcony. He climbed over the top as a door opened and a TRIO enforcer stepped outside.

The man gasped with surprise and tried to unsling his CAR-15. Trent's leg lashed out, raking the teeth of an *ashiko* across his opponent's abdomen. The hoodlum screamed as sharp spikes ripped into his guts. Trent closed in swiftly and clapped both hands to the man's head. The blades of his *shuko* punched through bone, piercing the man's skull to puncture his brain. Trent yanked the spikes free and let the sentry's corpse drop to the balcony, blood oozing down the man's face.

He yanked down the face mask to use his teeth as he hastily unfastened the straps to his "tiger claws." He discarded the *shuko* claws and quickly took the rope from his shoulder. Trent tied one end to the balcony, double knotting it to be certain the line would hold. He tossed the rope over the side as another TRIO goon appeared at the door.

The man held a Japanese Nambu pistol in his fist. Trent slashed a reverse roundhouse kick to the attacker's arm. The *ashiko* strapped to his foot slashed flesh from the thug's elbow to the back of his hand. The Nambu fell from bloodied fingers and the hoodlum opened his mouth to scream. Trent's hand flashed to the handle of his *ninja-do*. The sword hissed from its scabbard in a lightning-fast *kiai* draw. The blade slashed the TRIO man under the chin, slicing open his throat with a single stroke.

"You'd better get up there fast," Katz told Calvin

James. "Looks like our friend has already gotten himself in some trouble."

"Nothing he can't handle so far," the black warrior commented, but he rushed to the wall nonetheless.

James grabbed the rope and began climbing it hand over hand until he could brace his feet against the wall and "walk" up the surface. The former SEAL commando quickly scaled the building and climbed over the balcony while the other members of Phoenix Force moved into position, as well.

Katz and Manning moved to the rear of the temple. The Canadian demolitions expert ducked beneath a windowsill and carefully inserted a five-ounce charge of C-4 plastic explosives. He set a pencil-thin radio-operated detonator in the puttylike charge. Then Manning hurried to the thick oak doors at the back of the building and prepared a similar charge. The detonator was operated by a quartz battery and equipped with an individual timer. The Canadian set the timer for twenty seconds.

Manning and Katz found cover at the opposite side of the building. The C-4 exploded, blasting the door to kindling. Voices cried out in alarm and pain within the temple. An automatic weapon snarled, spraying the gap with copper-jacketed projectiles. There was no living target in the path of these bullets.

The Canadian demo pro unclipped a small radio transceiver from his belt and pressed a button. The transceiver emitted an ultrahigh frequency signal that activated the radio detonator in the C-4 charge under the windowsill.

Another violent explosion rocked the temple and blew the window to pieces. Shards of glass became flying shrapnel that showered the TRIO henchmen inside the building. Howls of agony blended with the echo of the blast as razor-sharp fragments sliced into human flesh.

Katz and Manning figured the enemy would keep their heads down for a second or two. They charged through the doorway, weapons ready for combat.

The Phoenix pair entered a large kitchen that had been transformed into a pile of wreckage and dusty debris by the explosions. Only a handful of survivors remained among the TRIO goons who had been unfortunate enough to be in the kitchen when Phoenix Force struck. All were dazed and bloodied, eardrums ruptured and skin lacerated by flying glass.

Three TRIO members still tried to raise their weapons and attack the Phoenix pair. Katz fired his Uzi, hosing the three men with 9mm slugs. Faces and chests were shredded by parabellum slugs. The hoodlums sprawled on the floor like three lumps of butchered beef.

Another thug reached for a .38 Smith & Wesson on the floor. Manning's boot slammed down on the man's hand, pinning it to the floor as he stamped the butt of his FLN rifle into the mastoid bone behind the guy's left ear. The hood uttered a sigh, almost an expression of relief, and slumped unconscious on his belly.

Suddenly a burly Chinese leaped up from the floor and struck out at Manning with a long curved knife. The blade slashed the Canadian's left forearm as he raised it to protect his throat. The man prepared to lunge with his weapon, but Manning quickly lashed the barrel of his FLN across his opponent's face.

The assailant stumbled backward into a wall. Manning braced the FLN rifle against his hip and triggered a 3-round burst. Several 7.62mm missiles caught the knife man squarely in the hollow of the throat. He dropped his blade and clasped both hands to his wounded neck as if somehow he could pull it back together again. The Chinese killer slumped to the floor, his eyes open wide as he stared into oblivion.

"How bad is your wound?" Katz asked, moving to Manning's side.

"Not as bad as his," the Canadian replied simply, tilting his head toward the dead Chinese. "Occupational hazard."

Blood pumped from the cut in Manning's forearm, dyeing his sleeve crimson. Katz stripped a black *obi* belt from a dead man's waist and took a wooden spoon from the sink. He helped Manning tie a tourniquet around the Canadian's forearm, using the belt and the long-handled spoon.

"That ought to reduce the bleeding until Calvin can take care of your arm," the Israeli remarked.

The roar of an explosion in another room trembled through the temple. No doubt about it. The rest of Phoenix Force had arrived.

20

Rafael Encizo and David McCarter had each lobbed SAS-style "flash-bang" grenades through windows at the front of the temple. The powerful twin-concussion blast that followed threw the oak doors open. One broke off its hinges and tumbled down the front steps.

"Knock, knock," McCarter muttered as he dashed through the entrance with his Ingram M-10 in his fists.

Encizo was right behind him, Heckler & Koch MP-5 ready for action. They charged into the main worship hall of the temple. The explosion had dazed the TRIO goons inside the massive room. Three men had been rendered unconscious, but almost a dozen were only stunned. Half of these were still on their knees, blood trickling from their ears and nostrils. The others had risen unsteadily to their feet, clutching an assortment of weapons that ranged from submachine guns to bladed instruments.

McCarter did not hesitate. He promptly aimed his machine pistol at the closest opponent who carried a firearm and squeezed the trigger. Parabellums riddled the gunman's upper torso. The impact hurled the thug into two other TRIO flunkies. All three fell to the tatami-covered floor.

Encizo reacted to danger in the same manner. The Cuban realized that ruthlessness is sometimes the only way to survive. He fired his MP-5, blasting a salvo into a pair of gun-toting goons. The pair were propelled backward and tripped over the body of a third man who was still on his knees.

The British warrior swung his M-10 toward another Oriental buttonman armed with a Beretta M-12. Both men opened fire, but McCarter's Ingram spoke a fragment of a second sooner. The TRIO gunsel jerked and twitched as bullets crashed into his chest. The aim of his Italian blaster was shifted away from McCarter and the man fired a volley of 9mm rounds into one of his comrades who had just drawn a Nambu pistol from shoulder leather.

A TRIO killer raised a Chinese *fu* hatchet and hurled it at Encizo. The Cuban weaved away from the hand-ax that whirled past his head. The handle tagged Encizo on the shoulder. His stomach contorted, but the Phoenix Force veteran had come close to death and terrible injury before. He controlled his fear and triggered the machine pistol, the 9mm shockers shredding the hatchet man's chest.

Four dazed TRIO flunkies tried to drag themselves to their feet. Encizo stepped forward and kicked one of them in the face, breaking several teeth and sending him back to dreamland. He chopped the side of his hand to the base of another guy's neck and knocked the second dolt unconscious.

McCarter backhanded the frame of his Ingram across the third diehard goon. Steel met skin and bone hard. Bone lost the contest and the man collapsed with a broken jaw. The fourth rose up behind McCarter, but the Briton suddenly launched a back "mule" kick and slammed a heel to the man's chest. The TRIO henchman flopped on his back and McCarter turned to step forward and swing the steel toe of his boot between the thug's splayed legs. The hoodlum shrieked and passed out.

The silence that followed was brief as more shooting resumed upstairs, but the fighting in the worship hall was over. Encizo gazed at the bronze Buddha at the opposite end of the room. Jasmine incense curled up from an ornate brass burner nearby. The rippling smoke seemed to alter the features of the statue. For a moment, Buddha appeared to shake his head as if saddened by the bloodshed that had taken place.

That makes two of us, the Cuban thought grimly as he swapped magazines to reload his Heckler & Koch machine pistol.

CALVIN JAMES AND JOHN TRENT had discovered a billet on the third story. The black warrior and the ninja burst through the entrance from the balcony and confronted seven startled TRIO hoodlums. The henchmen reached for their weapons and James opened fire.

A volley of 5.56mm slugs took out two TRIO flunkies before they could even aim their weapons. Bullets burned through flesh, shattered bone and dispatched the hoodlums to their ancestors. Their lifeless bodies tumbled across the sleeping mats on the floor as two other creeps at the opposite end of the room swung pistols toward James and Trent.

The ninja held his Colt Commander in one fist and a *metsubushi* in the other. The *metsubushi* was a hollowed-out eggshell filled with flashpowder and black pepper. Trent hurled the egg as he squeezed off his first shot and drilled a .45 slug through the center of a gunman's chest.

The *metsubushi* exploded on impact. A burst of white light and a cloud of flying paper assaulted the second gunman's face. Half-blind, he triggered his Nambu pistol and fired a 9mm round into the wall behind Trent. The ninja blasted a 185-grain lead messenger into the

TRIO goon's stomach. The thug fell against a wall and screamed as blood bubbled from his middle. Trent shot him again, pumping the next .45 slug in the man's heart.

Another gunner was slow to react and further affected by the ninja "sight remover" Trent had hurled. However, he still managed to claw open a button-flap holster and draw an old Walther P-38 autoloader. Trent had shifted his Commander to his left hand as he drew closer and swiftly pulled the *ninja-do* from its scabbard. The terrified hoodlum raised his German pistol as the ninja's sword flashed. Sharp steel chopped through flesh and bone. The man screamed as his gun hit the floor. His fist was still clamped around it. Blood gushed from the stump of his wrist as he dropped onto a mattress on the floor and began to slip into a state of shock.

The last two TRIO enforcers launched themselves at Calvin James. One man wielded a *wakazashi* short sword while the other attacked with his bare hands. The Phoenix pro concentrated on the greater threat and fired three rounds into the swordsman's upper body. The high-velocity blitzers sizzled clean through the aggressor, bursting his heart and severing the spinal cord. The swordsman collapsed, but his partner kept coming.

Strong hands grabbed the barrel of James's M-16. A snarling Japanese killer wrenched the assault rifle, trying to disarm the black hardcase. James did not intend to waste time playing tug-of-war with a lunatic. He suddenly launched a high tae kwon-do roundhouse kick. His boot slammed into the side of his opponent's head. The grip on the gun barrel slipped off as James pivoted with the motion of his kick.

The black man rammed the butt of his M-16 into the TRIO goon's abdomen, striking him under the heart. The hoodlum gasped and started to fold up from the blow. James hit him with a back fist to the right temple and the dude went down like a felled redwood.

"Okay," the black warrior said, breathing hard from exertion and stress. "Let's see what's happening downstairs."

TRIO had been vanquished everywhere in the temple except on the second story. McCarter and Encizo had charged up a flight of stairs to find a wide, empty room divided by a set of sliding rice-paper doors. Actually the room was not quite empty. Three TRIO killers were stationed there, manning an M-60 mounted machine gun. The two Phoenix Force commandos reached the head of the stairs and saw the big chopper.

They ducked just in time. A stream of 7.62 steel-jacketed hornets ripped air and splintered support beams above their heads. The pair were pinned down at the head of the stairs. Lobbing a grenade at the machine-gun nest would be dangerous since one of the TRIO hitmen could simply kick the blaster right back where it came from. McCarter and Encizo stayed down and tried to decide how to handle the slaughter team stationed on the second floor.

Calvin James and John Trent cautiously descended another flight of stairs and also discovered the machine gunners set up in the next room. However, James had no problem solving the predicament. He aimed his M-16 carefully and triggered the M-203 attachment.

The grenade launcher recoiled harshly, ramming the plastic stock of the assault rifle painfully against its owner. A 40mm projectile sailed into the middle of the machine-gun nest and exploded on impact. The blast tore the three hoodlums apart. Dismembered limbs and gory entrails were strewn across the room. The M-60 was smashed into a lump of twisted metal, its barrel snapped off from the frame.

The explosion also ripped down the rice-paper screen—much to the dismay of half a dozen TRIO agents who had been hidden behind it. Four of the hoodlums, including Harold Kuming and Andrew Tanaka, bolted through a door to the balcony. The other two had been bowled over by the blast. They rose to their knees and aimed their Beretta M-12 subguns at the upstairs flight of steps.

Their attention was momentarily turned away from the head of the other stairwell where Encizo and McCarter were still positioned. The British and Cuban warriors opened fire. The two TRIO gunmen twisted and gyrated as bullets smashed into their bodies. James contributed a burst of 5.56mm missiles to help the hoodlums find out if there is life after death.

"Hold your fire, Cal!" Encizo shouted. "We're coming up!"

"No sweat," James assured him as he took an empty mag from his M-16. "I'm reloading, anyway. Watch yourselves. Some of the bastards ducked onto the balcony."

Encizo and McCarter rushed from the head of the stairs to the ruins of the machine-gun nest. The Cuban saw the door leading to the balcony. The stubby muzzle of a Beretta M-12 stared back at him. Encizo retreated from the path of fire a moment before the enemy gunman squeezed the trigger.

Bullets slashed into a wall near the Cuban's position. He hit the floor and fired back as McCarter sent another volley of 9mm lead at the TRIO man's station. Projectiles tore chunks from the doorway and the gunman cried out as splinters pierced his face. The guy recoiled from the door and grabbed the handrail of the balcony. He fired one final burst at his opponents and swung a leg over the rail.

Then Encizo nailed him with a trio of parabellums in the rib cage. The impact hurled the gunman over the edge of the balcony, shrieking in terror and pain as he plunged two stories to the ground below.

McCarter rushed to the balcony and peered over the edge. He saw the broken corpse of the gunman below and three fleeing figures heading for the forest. One man turned and fired a pistol at the Briton. The bullet smacked into the framework of the balcony less than a foot from McCarter's left leg.

"Bloody turd," the Briton growled as he aimed his Ingram and fired the last five rounds from its magazine.

Two clods of dirt spat up from the ground near the pistolman's feet. At least one bullet struck its intended target. The gunman dropped his weapon and melted to the ground. The other two TRIO agents continued to run deeper into the forest.

"Silly blokes must have forgotten all about the cars parked around back," McCarter remarked.

"Probably figure they'd get wasted if they headed for the cars," Encizo commented. "And they're probably right. Yakov and Gary would nail anybody who entered the lot and tried to take one of the cars."

"Think we should go after them?" McCarter inquired.

"More dangerous than it's worth," Encizo replied. "We've crushed TRIO in San Francisco, taken care of that heroin cache and accomplished our mission. If those two are small fry, it's no big deal."

"And if they're not?" McCarter asked, raising an eyebrow.

"Then we'll probably get another shot at them again in the future," the Cuban stated. "I got a feeling we'll be seeing more of TRIO...."

"Holy shit!" Calvin James exclaimed.

McCarter and Encizo turned sharply and stared into the stern face of Yoshimitsu Ito. The samurai strode proudly forward, his *katana* thrust in an *obi* sash. Encizo pointed his MP-5 at Yoshimitsu, and McCarter yanked his Browning Hi-Power from shoulder leather.

"This time I do not run, yes?" Yoshimitsu announced with an arrogant smile. "The two half-breed scum will not criticize me in their memories, for they too fled when they knew the battle was lost."

"Well, you can tell us all about it later, mate," McCarter stated. "Put the sword on the floor and raise your hands...."

"A samurai never surrenders," Yoshimitsu spat. "And I refuse to willingly give up my *katana*. It is my soul and the soul of my fathers for two hundred years. I will surrender my soul only upon death."

"That can be arranged very easily," Encizo informed him.

"Death does not frighten me," Yoshimitsu declared. "My dreams of power and wealth are obviously ruined, so I have only one choice left. I shall die as a samurai, with sword in hand."

"You got it, asshole," Calvin James announced as he aimed his M-16 at Yoshimitsu. "As soon as you take that sucker outta its scabbard, we're gonna burn your ass. Is that honor or just plain stupid, man?"

"I do not..." Yoshimitsu suddenly glared at something he saw beyond Calvin James. "Ninja?"

"Hai," John Trent declared as he walked toward the samurai. *"Watakushi ninja kara Kaiju Uji, Yoshimitsu-san."*

Yoshimitsu seemed amused by Trent's statement. He uttered a long reply in Japanese. Trent simply nodded in reply and began to unstrap his shoulder holster.

"Wait a minute," Encizo insisted. "What the hell is this all about?"

"Yoshimitsu has given his word as a samurai that he is the last of our enemy left in this building," Trent replied as he handed the Colt Commander and shoulder leather to Calvin James. "He has also insulted my family and challenged me to a duel."

"Man, you gotta be kidding us." James sighed with exasperation.

"Look, we can't allow ourselves to get lured into personal matters," Encizo told Trent. "Yoshimitsu is more valuable alive."

"You won't take him alive," Trent explained. "Even if you wounded him and took him prisoner, he would swallow his own tongue before you could stop him. No, gentlemen, it is as Rafael said. Your missions is over. Yoshimitsu and I now have some personal business to settle. It is a matter of honor—a subject the colonel discussed earlier. I trust you understand."

"Have it your way, John," Encizo agreed reluctantly.

"Yoshimitsu-san," the ninja snapped as he drew his sword. *"Hajimaru!"*

"Hai," the samurai agreed, his *katana* flashing from its scabbard.

There were no polite, formal bows or polite gestures. Trent and Yoshimitsu attacked, swords slashing like dueling lightning bolts. Blades clanged as the combatants attacked and countered each other's strokes.

However, Yoshimitsu was armed with a longer sword of superior steel and craftsmanship. While the ninja's training includes numerous martial arts, Yoshimitsu had devoted his life to mastery of only one. He was clearly the better swordsman of the two.

Blades met again and both men pressed swords, their

faces grim as they breathed deeply into the *hara*, concentrating the *ki* or inner strength for their next moves. Suddenly they pushed each other away. Both men pivoted, but Yoshimitsu completed his turn first and slashed his *katana* across Trent's back. The ninja's speed and agility saved him from a crippling cut to the spine, but the wound was more than a mere nick. Blood oozed across the back of Trent's black jacket.

Trent blocked a sword stroke with the flat of his *ninja-do*. He attempted a backhand sweep, but Yoshimitsu expected this tactic and weaved out of the way. His *katana* slashed a shallow cut across Trent's left side. The samurai laughed as Trent jumped back, scarlet staining the front of his *gi*.

"Shit," James muttered, wishing he could come to his friend's assistance, but he realized Trent did not want this.

Steel clashed. Yoshimitsu suddenly twisted his wrists and the longer, curved blade of the *katana* seemed to wrap around the straight blade of the *ninja-do*. He turned fiercely and Trent's sword was yanked from his grasp. It sailed eight feet and fell to the floor near the remnants of the mangled M-60 machine gun.

Yoshimitsu swung a cross-body stroke, but Trent ducked under it. The samurai slashed a diagonal cut. To his surprise, steel clanged against steel. Trent had drawn a steel fan from his jacket. The ninja snapped the fan open as his opponent swung again.

Trent parried the blade with the metal ribs of his fan and quickly thrust a hook kick to his opponent's ribs. Yoshimitsu grunted and bellowed with anger as he attempted a sweep cut. Trent dodged the sword, jammed it with his fan and punted a side kick to Yoshimitsu's lower abdomen.

The samurai was too well trained to allow anger to

make him careless a second time. He swung his *katana* in two rapid strokes. The first was a feint, but the second sliced away a portion of the fan, cutting steel ribs as if they were Popsicle sticks. Trent snapped his wrist and hurled the fan at Yoshimitsu's face as if throwing a Frisbee. The samurai ducked in a reflex reaction while Trent dived to the floor and shoulder-rolled closer to his *ninja-do*.

Yoshimitsu raised his *katana* and charged. The ninja suddenly hurled an egg at the samurai's feet. The *metsubushi* exploded with a brilliant flash and spewed black pepper up at Yoshimitsu's face. The samurai retreated, blinking his eyes and shaking his head furiously.

Trent gathered up his *ninja-do*, holding it in a one-hand grip, the blade jutting from the bottom of his fist. He attacked, slashing the sword in a figure-eight pattern. The blades clanged as Yoshimitsu struggled to combat this unorthodox style of *ken-jutsu*.

Suddenly Trent shoved hard with both hands on the handle of his sword. The large square hand guard of his *ninja-do* had trapped the *katana* against the straight blade. Yoshimitsu grunted and hissed as he yanked and pushed. Then abruptly his sword was free and he raised the *katana* overhead.

Trent darted forward and stepped past the samurai, his fist held high. Blood dripped from the blade of his *ninja-do*. He had slashed a deep wound in Yoshimitsu's right armpit. The samurai stood frozen for a moment as crimson poured down the side of his *gi* jacket. Slowly he lowered his arms. The *katana* slipped from his fingers and he dropped to his knees, head bowed in submission.

"*Omedeto gozaimas,*" he whispered. "Congratulations."

"*Domo arigato,*" Trent replied as he raised the *ninja-do* in a two-hand grip. "Thank you very much."

With that, he swung the sword and chopped off Yoshimitsu Ito's head. The decapitated body fell on its side, blood spilling across the floor.

"Well," Encizo said with a sigh. "I guess that wraps up everybody's business. Let's go home."

MORE GREAT ACTION COMING SOON

PHOENIX FORCE

#18 Night of the Thuggee
Passage to Hell

Americans are dying in India, and an ancient cult of professional assassins known as the Thuggees are staging a deadly return performance. But this time they're being directed by the KGB, who are manipulating the Thugs into doing their dirty work. Phoenix Force takes their show on the road and travels to India to confront the most dangerous and efficient secret society to wield a silken garrote.

Will this be the Force's closing act?

Mack Bolan's
PHOENIX FORCE
by Gar Wilson

Schooled in guerrilla warfare, equipped with all the latest lethal hardware, Phoenix Force battles the powers of darkness in an endless crusade for freedom, justice and the rights of the individual. Follow the adventures of one of the legends of the genre. Phoenix Force is the free world's foreign legion!

"Gar Wilson is excellent! Raw action attacks the reader on every page."

—*Don Pendleton*

Phoenix Force titles are available wherever paperbacks are sold.

GOLD EAGLE

Mack Bolan's

ABLE TEAM

by Dick Stivers

Action writhes in the reader's own street as Able Team's Carl "Mr. Ironman" Lyons, Pol Blancanales and Gadgets Schwarz make triple trouble in blazing war. To these superspecialists, justice is as sharp as a knife. Join the guys who began it all—Dick Stivers's Able Team!

"This guy has a fertile mind and a great eye for detail. Dick Stivers is brilliant!"

—*Don Pendleton*

Able Team titles are available wherever paperbacks are sold.

GOLD EAGLE

GET THE NEW WAR BOOK AND MACK BOLAN BUMPER STICKER FREE!

Mail this coupon today!